HVZA 3

Hudson Valley
Zombie Apocalypse

Project Decimation

Written by
Linda Zimmermann

For videos, podcasts, and information on HVZA and the HVZA graphic novel go to:

www.hvzombie.com and click on Zombies

HVZA logo by Big Guy Media and Ryan Browne

Zombie makeup on cover created by:
Michael Worden SFX, michaeljworden.com

Cover Art by Gordon Bond Designs, gordon@gordonbonddesigns.com

Copyright © 2018 Linda Zimmermann

www.gotozim.com

Eagle Press
ISBN: 978-1-937174-20-0

Author's Note

HVZA 3 has been a long time coming. I began it a few years ago and while the majority of the plot was formed in my head from the start, getting it on paper took an inordinate amount of time, for a variety of reasons.

Several other book projects took over my life for a couple of years, but still, when time allowed, I returned to my zombie apocalypse world. Then there was the small matter of the life-threatening medical ordeal which put quite a damper on my productivity, but still, when I was able, I returned to my zombies.

Finally, as 2017 was drawing to a close, I said enough is enough: I have zombies to kill and people to save, so I ceased all other projects to concentrate on Becks, zombie parasites, and a New York City and Hudson Valley full of mayhem, tragedy, and eternal hope.

No matter what else I do in my varied career, for me, nothing compares to immersing myself in my own fictional universes. I live in that universe night and day, and when I write those final two words—The End—I feel both happy that I have completed the story, and sad that I have to leave it and return to reality (or as close to reality as I am capable of getting!).

I hope *HVZA 3* pulls you in and takes you on a wild ride. If you find yourself saying, "Holy crap, this is so realistic!" and end up losing sleep over it, my job is done! Ultimately, though, I hope this book provides you with some escapist entertainment in a manner that only a herd of zombies headed straight for you can provide.

Linda Zimmermann
Hudson Valley of New York
March 2018

Acknowledgements

It's hard to believe, but it was way back in 1998 when Gordon Bond created my first ghost book cover. He is now an author of several books, and you would think the two of us would know better by now, but here we are twenty years later doing the same things again!

Thank you, Gordon, for an amazing cover that really captures the world of *HVZA*!

As for Michael Worden, police officer, author, and special effects artist, may we have many more sessions where you glue bald caps to my scalp and flesh wounds to my face, and cover my skin in a lovely palette of decomp colors and fake blood.

Then there is my husband, Robert Strong, who tirelessly goes with me on my scouting and research trips, proofreads, and generally manages to deal with all of the quirks and eccentricities of a zombie novelist. (Especially one who has been known to jump out of the bushes in full zombie makeup to freak him out.)

And to all of the *HVZA* fans who have supported my work and encouraged (and sometimes badgered, in a good way) me to continue the series—many, many thanks. Becks and I couldn't have done it without you!

Chapter 1

The first undead corpse in Manhattan attempting to cross the makeshift footpath at the base of the remnants of the George Washington Bridge slipped and fell into the muddy waters of the Hudson River, adding his body to the tight web of debris. The next two or three hundred zombies trying to get across also failed to make it, and their torsos, arms, legs, and heads slowly filled in the gaps in the path, also helping to widen it. Finally, a petite female zombie who used to serve coffee and pastries at a small shop in the garment district—who still had her soiled, blue and white striped waitress cap pinned to her tangle of blond hair, and a crooked name tag that read, "Tammy"—successfully walked the entire length and stepped onto the soil of New Jersey.

The center span of the bridge had been blown out by the Army in the early days of the infection—along with the other bridges and tunnels to Manhattan—in order to keep the millions of fresh zombies contained on the island. For several months, the river was still navigable by boat if you had a small craft and stuck to the shore lines. But over a year of logs and a remarkable variety of debris coming down the river had formed a sort of dam along the fallen superstructure of steel and concrete, coupled with the many cars and trucks that had packed the bridge when it was demolished.

Water was still able to flow under and through this snarled mass, but silt, leaves, sticks, logs, derelict boats, bodies, and bones gradually accumulated until the dam stretched the width of the river and formed an embankment from shore to shore. As much as zombies hated being near water, their hunger drove them to seek out new sources of food, and therefore this new link to fresh hunting grounds was an opportunity that their single-minded neural networks simply could not resist.

Limping and awkwardly swinging her long-dead limbs along the river road that passed the boat docks, Tammy slowly followed the twisting and turning pavement and ascended onto the Palisades Interstate Parkway. From there, it would be an easy walk through northern New Jersey into Rockland County, New York, and its many roads and highways that spread out through the Hudson Valley.

Unfortunately for zombie Tammy, but fortunately for the few remaining inhabitants of southern Rockland County, a patrol dispatched

1

the lone walking corpse with a single headshot that splattered blood and brains all over her waitress cap.

However, it would not be so easy to kill the other hundreds of thousands of zombies that began to follow in Tammy's footsteps.

Chapter 2

Six weeks after being rescued from the zombie hell of the New Jersey suburbs, Dr. Rebecca "Becks" Truesdale was only waking up screaming two or three times a night.

While her physical wounds had healed nicely since she was brought back to West Point, her mental and emotional states were still far from the confident, kick-ass loner she had transformed herself into when the zombie apocalypse made civilization crumble. Becks had learned to survive and kill—both zombies and humans—and had changed in more ways than she ever imagined possible.

However, the long months of her horrific ordeal—much of which time she was injured and isolated—had also taken its toll. It was a delayed reaction, though, as only after she was safe, eating well, taking hot showers, and sleeping in a warm bed for a couple of weeks, did the terror of all her experiences start bubbling up like a hot magma burning through her heart and soul.

"It's okay, Baby. It's okay. I'm here," Cam whispered as he wrapped his arms tightly around Becks' trembling body after she sat bolt upright and screamed at the top of her lungs for the second time in as many hours.

When her nightmares began, Cam insisted on sleeping with her so she didn't wake up alone. He would hold her, stroke her hair, kiss her gently on the forehead, and speak to her in a soothing and reassuring voice. Becks hated these bouts of fear, which she perceived as a weakness, but she also was so very grateful to have Cam by her side again. A strong hug and a few words from him made all the scenes of blood and gore she was reliving in her dreams fade away—at least for an hour or so.

The doctors at West Point offered her sedatives and sleeping pills, but Becks was just stubborn enough to refuse any sort of medication which she believed would only mask the symptoms of the psychological issues she had to deal with in her own way. Of course, as a doctor, she knew all too well the effects of Post-Traumatic Stress Disorder, of which she was exhibiting classic signs, but Becks was still too mired in the trauma to the think clearly enough to ask for help.

So what if she had to hide in a drainpipe surrounded by zombies, slaughter them in brutal hand-to-hand fighting, shoot, stab, and burn people alive, eat rats, battle the bitter cold temperatures and snow, and literally run for her life, time and time again? She simply did what she had to, to survive, and her subconscious would just have to grow a virtual 'pair' and deal with it.

Working in a lab again certainly helped. Back with her test tubes, Petri dishes, and instruments, Becks was in her happy place from the moment she slipped on her lab coat. It also helped to be working side by side with Phil again. He had endured his own personal hell, losing most of his family and being imprisoned with thousands of zombies, but he now seemed as content and good-humored as he had been back at ParGenTech, BZA (Before the Zombie Apocalypse). If both he and his son—who had witnessed his mother, sister, and grandparents murdered and eaten—could emerge from the depths of their despair, then she could, too.

There was certainly enough work to keep her mind occupied. While she had been gone, some of the doctors and scientists at West Point had been trying to develop a vaccine to the Zombie Infection Parasites, or ZIPs. Parasite vaccines were one of the more difficult medical challenges BZA, and now AZA (After the Zombie Apocalypse), with limited resources and staff, it often seemed like an impossible dream, but it didn't mean they would not keep trying.

BZA, there had been some promising experiments with some early-stage parasites being irradiated so that they were unable to reproduce. When these sterile parasites were injected into the bloodstream, they provoked immunological responses which researchers hoped would protect the host from future infections from non-sterile parasites. It was a longshot to produce a vaccine for the complex and adaptable ZIPs, but it would be a crucial step for the survival of mankind, which at this point was very much in doubt, given the current global situation. Could the world ever recover from the loss of billions of people?

"I don't know about the rest of the world, but life at the Point seems pretty damn good at the moment," Cam said, a second before sinking his teeth into the crispy skin of a piece of fried chicken.

He and Becks sat in the expansive mess hall after her shift in the lab, but while he relished every delicious bite, she was clearly a million miles away and not so much eating as pushing her food around her plate.

"What?" Becks asked, not having heard a word.

4

"I said I booked us two seats on the next flight to Paris, because I feel like having croissants for breakfast," Cam said to see if she was listening.

"Oh, that's fine," she replied mechanically.

For her own good, Cam flipped a spoonful of mashed potatoes at her, which stuck quite nicely to her cheek.

"Cam, what the hell!?" Becks protested, wiping her face with a napkin as she tried to decide whether to be pissed or amused.

"Trues, you are somewhere out in space, no doubt thinking of ZIPs, modifying genes, and god knows what, when you should just be enjoying this fabulous meal and conversing with your charming and devilishly handsome dinner companion."

"You're right, I am sorry," she said, seemingly reaching out to take his hand, but instead, wiping the sticky lump of thrown potato down his arm.

Had they been alone or back at Cam's compound in Saugerties, a full-on food fight would have ensued, but given their surroundings and the crazy level of discipline everywhere at West Point, they had to content themselves with exchanging hushed threats.

Becks finally ate and enjoyed her meal. Then she and Cam took a lovely walk in the warm evening air along the river, and life did seem pretty damn good at that moment. However, a solitary figure desperately paddling up the river on a raft constructed out of office furniture and empty plastic bottles would soon shatter that peace of mind.

Chapter 3

Dr. Martin Devereaux was universally disliked by both students and faculty during his almost four decades at the Columbia University College of Physicians and Surgeons in New York City, because of his gruff demeanor and generally mean-spirited behavior.

Dr. Martin Devereaux was also universally admired and respected for his unrivaled genius, and he had often been described as having one of the most brilliant medical minds to ever grace the planet. No one could stand to be in the same room with him, yet countless people were indebted to Devereaux for either their careers or their very lives, as his research and discoveries had launched so many new medications, treatments, and technologies that there wasn't a modern hospital in the world that wasn't employing some technique that had been born in his fertile mind. Statues should have been erected in his honor and he should have been celebrated in every country—if only everyone didn't hate his guts so much.

Devereaux didn't give a damn how many people hated him. In fact, the more the better, as it spared him having to waste time with banal social interactions. He was thus free to concentrate on his work—the work of curing diseases and saving lives, which certainly must rank higher than being able to chit chat at fundraisers and cocktail parties.

Nothing in his character or in his past mattered now, however, as he sat in his office which looked west toward the Hudson River. He had so far survived the chaos, turmoil, and bloodshed of the zombie apocalypse, predominantly because he was so clever. That, and he had a group of about three dozen students and faculty to help protect him and gather supplies. That number had been cut in half since the bridges and tunnels were destroyed and they were all trapped on Manhattan, but the fact that more than a dozen of them were still left alive after all this time was truly remarkable under such dire circumstances.

To his credit, Devereaux recognized the fact that these brave young men and women continued to risk their lives in order for him to stay alive and keep his research going. While he never actually thanked any of them—except on a single occasion—he did make a concerted effort to not treat them like dirt under his feet. It wasn't easy, but it was the least he could do, as these people had sacrificed their chances of getting off Manhattan to stick with him.

His own poor health prevented Devereaux from making a run for it when word began to spread that the bridges and tunnels were being rigged with explosives. He had been scheduled for heart surgery in the early days of infection, but his surgeon was one of the first to get bitten and turn zombie. As conditions rapidly deteriorated and medical priorities even more rapidly shifted to perpetual emergencies, he never received that operation. Initially, people joked that Devereaux's surgery had been canceled because they discovered he actually didn't have a heart, but with the devastating onslaught of the zombie apocalypse, no one was laughing for long.

Devereaux's condition had steadily worsened and he did his best to keep working, but he knew better than anyone that without that surgery he wouldn't live very long. He then reached a point where he realized that even surgery would no longer help. But that was only part of why he sent one of his students on the risky mission up the river. After a recent scouting mission, the students reported enormous herds of zombies converging on the remnants of the George Washington Bridge, and that they were actually starting to cross the river on piles of debris.

They knew the military was still functional in some capacity, as helicopters had been spotted several times in the past few weeks. They were seen traveling south down the river and then veering west toward northern New Jersey. Devereaux had surmised that they were most likely based at West Point—at least he hoped so. He also hoped that they may have some doctors who could carry on his important work.

He did not easily come to the decision to send a young man out on a possibly fatal mission, but time was not on the side of mankind. If there was still an army, they needed to know that legions of the undead were marching their way toward the Hudson Valley. They also needed to know that he was dying, and that he just might have the answer to turn the tide of the zombie apocalypse. The outside world needed to know about Project Decimation, before it was too late for him, and too late for everyone else still breathing.

Chapter 4

The fact that Dr. Phillip Masterson had packed on more than 30 pounds over the winter spoke to the high standard of living at West Point, which allowed such a high caloric intake when most of the survivors in the outside world were starving. What had begun as stress eating at the word of Becks' suspected death, spiraled into frequent binges of comfort food. That, along with 12 to 18-hour work days, six days a week, meant that he had officially crossed the line of being just pleasingly plump.

So, as Phil ran down the hallway toward the lab, huffing and puffing, he felt every one of those extra pounds weighing him down. He made a pledge right then and there to get back into shape—if he and everyone else in the Hudson Valley survived long enough to start working out.

"Everyone...Attention...Please!" he shouted in between gasping breaths.

Becks, along with the other 20 staff members working that shift, instantly fell silent and stopped what they were doing. Some were so startled by Phil's state of alarm that they literally dropped what they were doing as several pieces of glassware hit the floor and shattered. Fortunately, none of the vessels contained anything *too* toxic or infectious.

As everyone rushed over to Phil, he took a moment to lean over and catch his breath, hands on knees, before he continued.

"There's some news...*big*...news," he said, still breathing heavily. It took a while, but finally Phil was able to share the shocking details of what had transpired in the last few hours. A Rockland County Militia patrol had spotted someone coming up the river on a raft made from some metal desk parts and empty water bottles and milk containers. He claimed to have come from the Columbia medical school with word that Dr. Martin Devereaux had developed something very important to fight the zombies.

Three more pieces of glassware hit the floor.

At this point, Becks and the other researchers gasped almost as loudly as Phil had from running. She and several others had either taken his classes or attended some of Devereaux's lectures over the years, and all of them knew of both his miserable reputation and astonishing accomplishments.

"I knew it. He's too mean of a son of a bitch to die," muttered one of the Army doctors who obviously had firsthand experience with Devereaux, but the doctor immediately regretted his snide remark after Phil continued.

"Well, Devereaux *is* dying, and he needs to get the details of his discovery out to the world and into the hands of the people who can use it. I'm not sure what it's all about, but they are bringing this man and some files here, to West Point, to us. He should be here within the hour."

"That's wonderful news!" someone exclaimed, as everyone else chimed in, until Phil silenced them in an ominous tone and then finished the story.

"That was the good news. The bad news is *very* bad, I'm afraid."

Phil went on to describe the makeshift bridge over which tens of thousands of zombies, if not more, were crossing and pouring northward every day. Everything they had fought for to clear and secure the Hudson Valley could be lost if these hordes continued unchecked. The Army was dispatching a helicopter on a reconnaissance mission, but if the information was even half accurate, they didn't have nearly the manpower or resources to combat those numbers of zombies. The spring offensive in northern New Jersey was currently well underway, and even if they pulled out all of those troops they would still be vastly outnumbered.

Becks' right hand reached under her lab coat so she could feel the reassuring grip of her Smith and Wesson 629 .44 magnum. No one else in the lab carried a weapon, but she was never without her pistol and a commando knife, even though she was at a highly fortified military base where just about everyone else was armed. She even hung her holster on the inside of the shower door in a plastic bag so it was always within reach, and both the pistol and the knife were under her pillow as she slept. Cam and Phil viewed this behavior as the obvious result of her PTSD, but she just saw it as common sense, or like extensions of her own body.

The next hour was filled with wild speculation and intense anxiety as they awaited the arrival of the mystery man. The news that Devereaux was still alive was nothing short of a bombshell, and they all wondered out loud how the anti-ZIPs projects would have benefited from his genius—while silently all giving thanks he hadn't been with them the last year to poison the comradery and *esprit de corps* with his acrimonious personality.

9

Becks simultaneously admired and despised Devereaux, both the result of the one class she had taken with him. No teacher had ever inspired her so much with his brilliant insights and staggering intellect. And no teacher had ever pissed her off so much when he gave her a C on her term paper.

Up to that point in her medical school career, she had never produced as fine a paper with such original and innovative research she had personally conducted, and she was crushed when he brutally criticized her methodology and conclusions—both of which were exemplary in the eyes of everyone else who read it. But there was no arguing with the high and mighty Devereaux, and that C remained the worst grade of her academic career, and it still made her blood boil whenever she thought of it.

Obviously, there were more important things to worry about now, so Becks would have to let bygones be bygones, especially if Devereaux had a solution to the zombie apocalypse. Still, if it came down to Devereaux saving mankind, or apologizing for giving her a bad grade for a great paper, she would have to seriously consider her options...

Chapter 5

Sticky Pete was Devereaux's obvious choice for the mission. Peter Hernandez was young, strong, and a former All-State track star. He had been a student in the biomedical engineering program at Columbia when the zombie shit hit the fan, and with no family to run to, he decided to stay with Devereaux, even when the university was being evacuated.

Sticky Pete was no stranger to loss, even before the apocalypse. His mother was a bond trader killed on 9/11 in the south tower, and his dad had died in Afghanistan during Pete's freshman year. His father had sustained numerous shrapnel wounds, any one of which wasn't very serious, but altogether they proved fatal due to massive blood loss which couldn't be staunched in the field. It was that day that Sticky Pete switched his intended field of study to bioadhesives, specifically designed for closing wounds until the patient could receive proper medical attention. His new nickname soon followed.

Despite his being the youngest of the group of students and faculty that remained, he had become the de facto leader of the group. He was adept at scavenging for supplies, and no one was ever lost or bitten on a mission he led. Sticky Pete was a survivor's survivor, and he even had the distinction of receiving the one and only compliment anyone had ever heard from Devereaux's lips. After single-handedly killing more than two dozen zombies and running over 30 blocks while carrying 40 pounds of much needed food and supplies, Devereaux had actually said, "Nice work, Pete."

As Devereaux's health deteriorated and the massive herds started converging on the George Washington Bridge, which was just a short distance from where they all worked and lived, plans emerged to construct something that would float on the river and could be propelled with a makeshift paddle. The craft also needed to be light and maneuverable enough to be carried 20 blocks north through heavily zombie-infested streets to get to the river bank past the collapsed George Washington Bridge obstruction.

When Sticky Pete was a kid, his parents had taken him to see the incredibly huge Spruce Goose plane that Howard Hughes had built. He remembered that Hughes had filled the massive wings with inflated beach balls so the plane wouldn't sink if there was a catastrophic failure as it tried to take off from the water. While Columbia University College of Physicians and Surgeons was fresh out of beach balls, the survivor group had amassed quite a pile of empty plastic containers, which when strapped to a couple of desktops and drawers that Sticky Pete had managed to glue together—to no one's surprise—he had a lightweight and serviceable raft.

If they could get it to the river, and if the water was calm, and if the tide was right and flowing north (one of their group knew that the Hudson was actually a tidal estuary which flows both ways), and if the glue remained intact, Sticky Pete just might be able to paddle far enough upriver for someone to notice him, or for him to find some sign of survivors on shore.

The first stage of the mission was the most dangerous, as it appeared as if every undead corpse in Manhattan was headed for the upper west side. Of course, the zombies didn't know they would be crossing the river into fresh hunting grounds, they only knew they were starving and would follow their herds anywhere for fresh meat.

The Columbia group had often employed motion detectors to create a distraction, and using slingshots from the rooftops, they were able to propel the shrieking devices to strategic locations to keep the herds concentrated just south of their position. The seven raft team members, including Sticky Pete, then dashed out of a service entrance carrying the raft. The other six in the group were composed of the best shooters and fighters, and their skills were called upon almost immediately.

Lone stragglers and small groups of three or four zombies were everywhere. The team would run 100 yards or so, drop the raft, and kill the zombies in their path. Avoiding gunfire when possible, their best weapon was "Mad Max" Rukowski, a little fireplug of a man with biceps the size of Christmas hams. He wielded a combination spiked club/axe he named Mama, after his overbearing mother, whom his father constantly referred to as the "Old Battle Axe."

Every time Mama cleaved a zombie skull in two, the cracking and splintering sounds made Max laugh like a maniac, hence his nickname. BZA, he was a semester away from graduating from the school of dentistry, but everyone agreed he had now found his true calling.

"I really would have sucked as a dentist," Mad Max even freely admitted.

Another deadly member of the team was Erin, who had been a second-year med student hoping to specialize in prosthetic limbs and rehabilitation. Since high school, she also had a penchant for creating odd mechanical devices. BZA, Erin had used her skills to make bizarre steampunk contraptions with profusions of whirring gears and ratcheting levers. She had made really good money on eBay and at the numerous steampunk conventions with her whimsical inventions, and had even considered giving up medicine to work on these gadgets full time—until zombies changed all of her plans.

AZA, it wasn't too much of a stretch to turn her talents into making weapons. Her favorite was "King George," fashioned to look like a regal scepter, with a twist—a very deadly twist. By pulling back a sliding bolt mechanism, a powerful spring was cocked and ready to propel a solid, stainless steel rod, ground to a sharp point.

Gracefully wielding King George as if she was about to knight a member of the undead, "Lady Erin," as she called herself, released the bolt at just the right moment to send the rod crashing through the cranium with the ease and effectiveness of dropping a brick on an egg. The relatively quiet weapon could then be cocked again in a second and ready to "knight" the next victim.

Then there was Margo, a stout, fair-complexioned girl who had been a sophomore at the onset of infection. She wasn't the brightest student, but she was pigheaded enough to study harder and longer than anyone, and so had managed to get decent grades. She claimed that the trait came naturally to her, as she grew up on a pig farm in Iowa, which is also where she learned to shoot. Margo was determined to become a doctor so she would never have to go back to that stinking patch of mud called home. Now, AZA, she yearned to be back on the family farm.

"Just give me one hour," she often said with real emotion in her voice, which pulled on one's heart strings until she revealed her motive. "It's not that I care to see my crazy family or that dilapidated house again, I just want to butcher a few hogs and eat pork until I burst!"

Unfortunately for her, and the rest of the group, rats and pigeons supplied their only source of meat. And even the rats were almost nonexistent now, as the zombie hordes had practically devoured the entire population.

As the raft team stopped to confront a group of about twenty zombies stretched out across the street, Margo raised her rifle and methodically began to pick them off as if it was a carnival game, despite the plan to be as quiet as possible.

"This little piggy went to market," she said, squeezing the trigger for her first shot which echoed through streets, before continuing her nursery rhyme with each successive shot. "This little piggy stayed home—"

"Do you really have to say that *every* time you shoot these things?" Max complained, an instant before swinging Mama down through the top of an elderly man's head, clean through to his nearly toothless jaw, and then laughing maniacally.

"Do *you* have to laugh like a hyena *every* time you split a skull?" she shouted back angrily.

The two didn't get along, and when it looked like they were more interested in fighting one another than killings zombies, Sticky Pete asserted his authority and got the team to focus on the task at hand. The long, cold winter had taken its toll on everyone's nerves, and Pete was actually surprised there hadn't been any homicides.

Pete's weapon of choice was a homemade spear, of sorts. He had welded a sturdy, large-gauge cannula—like a massive hypodermic needle—to the end of a metal curtain rod. He used it to great effect to pierce the eye sockets of zombies and poke a big hole in the network of ZIPs enveloping the human brains.

It was a technique Becks had perfected in New Jersey with the spears she had made with a broom handle, a hockey stick, and infomercial knife sets. They allowed for silent kills that saved precious ammunition, but there was nothing quiet about the raft team's desperate journey to get to the Hudson River.

The three remaining members of the raft team, Jiang, Josh, and Arjun, were the relatively more athletic individuals in the DNS—Devereaux's Nerd Squad. They weren't as eccentric and flamboyant as Mad Max, Lady Erin, and Margo, and they carried simple homemade spears and clubs for their quieter kills. They also had a full complement of various handguns, rifles, and shotguns for when circumstances called for raw firepower. In the beginning of the zombie crisis it was all completely overwhelming, considering their previous academic lifestyles, but it was remarkable how survival instincts quickly turned unassuming bookworms into efficient and ruthless killers.

There was a very close call about a block from the river when the team encountered a pack of about three dozen zombies. Arjun tossed one of their diversion spheres—a fanciful name for a tennis ball in which they had embedded flashing LED lights and a beeper, duct taped to a battery—but the ravenous zombies would not be distracted from the prospect of seven walking meat feasts.

Normally, Sticky Pete would have called for a V-formation to fight their way through the weakest section of the line and then run like hell, but the bulky raft changed the game. Directing Max and Erin to cover their flanks, the rest of them shifted positions and used the raft as a battering ram to punch a hole on the far left side of the street, where some cars helped slow down the other zombies' pursuit. One lanky zombie wearing a New York City sanitation department uniform managed to grab Pete's ankle after the raft had knocked his decaying body to the pavement, but Erin jumped to his defense and King George quickly shattered the back of the zombie's skull.

Once past the pack, they all resumed carrying the raft and made it safely to the water's edge, where no zombie cared to be without a really good reason. Of course, the living humans were the best reasons of all, and slowly, but relentlessly, every straggler in the neighborhood was headed their way.

"Hurry, we only have a few minutes," Pete shouted, as they struggled to maneuver the unwieldy raft down a steep embankment covered in foul-smelling muck.

Both Josh and Jiang tripped and fell to their knees, but kept their grasp on the raft. However, the last few feet were deceptively slippery and they all slid and tumbled into the river. Fortunately, the raft landed upright. Regaining their feet, they all waded out into waist-deep water and carefully examined the raft for any signs of leaks. When it appeared as if the special waterproof adhesive Sticky Pete had formulated was holding, he pulled himself up into the surprisingly seaworthy craft and unstrapped the makeshift paddle from his back. By this point, dozens of zombies had gathered at the top of the embankment, and he hesitated to start paddling.

15

"I can't leave you guys like this—" he started to protest, but the other six team members responded by giving the raft a mighty shove with all their strength, sending him on his way.

"Paddle like hell, Pete," Max yelled. "And don't look back."

"DNS can take care of themselves!" Josh shouted, although there was far more fear than conviction in his voice.

"Get the hell out of here and go save the world," Arjun added for good measure.

Pete started paddling as fast as he could, and after a few minutes he did stop looking back. His team had tried wading further up the river where there weren't as many reanimated corpses waiting for them, but the sounds of gunfire still spoke to the fierce fighting that ensued. The shots eventually became sporadic, and then stopped altogether, but he had no way of knowing if that meant that the DNS team had escaped or perished.

He paddled even harder, tears filling his eyes, determined to make this mission a success. Passing along the beautiful, steep cliffs of the palisades that lined the west bank of the river, he wondered why he never took the time to enjoy the Hudson Valley, but pain soon engulfed his thoughts. Blisters swelled up on his hands, but he kept paddling. Even after the blisters had torn open and his hands were raw, he paddled through the night and into the next morning.

Around midday, he stopped long enough for some water and a bag of trail mix—and to relieve himself into the river—but at that instant he realized the current was now flowing back down toward New York City, so he started paddling furiously again, using strips of his T-shirt as bandages on his hands. Finally, mercifully, as evening approached and every muscle in his body was wracked in searing pain, he heard voices from a long pier jutting out into the west bank of the river.

Praying they weren't scavengers, he turned toward them, stopping within shouting distance until he was able to ascertain that the men were part of some patrol and wanted to help. An hour later, he was sitting on a velvet settee in the parlor of a lovely old Victorian home in Piermont, New York. His hands had been properly bandaged, and his stomach was full of canned ham and fresh vegetables. While eating, he had told his story three separate times to people of increasing authority, and was then assured that West Point had been contacted and someone would be picking him up shortly.

It was all so surreal—almost as though the world hadn't changed here—and Pete wasn't entirely convinced he wasn't hallucinating, until a convoy of Army Humvees came roaring into the driveway.

Chapter 6

The ride up the Palisades Interstate Parkway was like something out of a crazy time machine story. The convoy passed futuristic-looking, anti-zombie weaponry on the backs of flatbed trucks, several farmers with horse-drawn wagons, and even a couple of soccer moms chauffeuring kids in SUVs.

"Would somebody please tell me what the hell is going on?" he asked the Humvee full of Army officers. "Do you still even have zombies here?"

The colonel in charge was so anxious to question Pete about his research that he forgot that the poor man had been isolated on Manhattan since the bridges were blown, and he didn't have a clue as to what was going on. The colonel offered a quick and concise summary of the dire straits down south, and in all the warm and temperate countries of the world.

He then spoke specifically about the Hudson Valley and how it had been completely overrun –leaving only West Point as a beacon of hope in the resurrection of civilization. He failed to mention the brave and resilient bands of survivors who had been left on their own and had done the vast majority of fighting and dying, but overinflating military glory was certainly not something new, even in the era of zombies.

The important thing was that thanks to bioweapons and a variety of treatments, the zombie tide—where the apocalypse had all begun—had been turned and life was returning and humans were making a comeback. There were clinics, schools, farms, some manufacturing, and marketplaces to buy, sell, and trade just about anything. Thanks to the Indian Point nuclear power plant, electricity was even returning to more and more communities every day. It was almost comical to watch people scream and react in shock and delight when a light suddenly came on, or they heard the hum of their refrigerator for the first time in over a year.

Pete listened to all the news with a mixture of joy and grief, as well as hope and regret. Was it wrong to have stayed at Columbia, facing unspeakable hardships, while keeping Devereaux and his discoveries out of the hands of the people who could have been using them against the zombie hordes? But what if they had tried to extract Devereaux and had failed? And how could they have known what was happening in the Hudson Valley?

Within 24 hours of the bridges and tunnels being destroyed, every ferry, yacht, barge, kayak, and inflatable raft on the island of Manhattan had taken off carrying those who either had the most money or the most guns. Thousands had died fighting for a spot on one of those vessels, and many more were lost as ships were sunk by severe overcrowding.

In the days and months that followed, clever individuals built crude rafts, but if they were able to carry these makeshift lifeboats to the river without getting bitten, or mugged by the living, they were often in for just as much trouble on the New Jersey side, as things went downhill fast there, too. Brooklyn, Queens, the Bronx, and Staten Island weren't any better.

The most athletic amongst the Manhattanites were able to swim across the river in the warmer weather, and a few others used ropes and their mountaineering skills to traverse the collapsed superstructures of the bridges, but they also encountered the same undead welcoming committees wherever they went.

Pete heard shooting as they drove past some houses about 100 yards from the highway, and he instinctively reached for his pistol, but the colonel just as quickly placed a firm hand on his arm to keep the pistol down.

"Just doing some routine cleanup," the colonel said calmly, as if he was talking about something mundane like the weather, but he realized that Pete's look of alarm and concern demanded further explanation.

Obviously, in order to declare any location safe and secure, *every* zombie needed to be eliminated. Gone were the days when it was acceptable to have zombies closed up in a house or car. Too many people had been infected or killed scavenging for supplies or looking for a new home to try to start their lives over. Now, unless a green checkmark was spray painted on the front door, you had to assume that nothing but infection and death awaited you inside.

Teams had been organized throughout the Hudson Valley to go through every structure and vehicle on every square inch of land. It was painstaking and dangerous work, but when everyone followed the rules it became quite routine, and even boring—until those moments of terror when you actually had to open that closet door, or go into the creepy

19

basement and pray that nothing jumped out at you. But that was the final step in the routine.

First, you pounded on the front door and made a racket, and then looked and listened for any signs of the undead. For those places that were obviously occupied, a small hole—about 2 inches in diameter—was drilled through the door. Poisoned meat was then dropped into the hole and the date and time was written in red marker next to it.

Only after the poison was given at least a full 72 hours to work, would the teams open the door to that building, but they still wouldn't enter. Small drones with cameras were then flown through the structure, giving the team a heads-up on the layout, what doors were closed, and if there were any bodies, to make damn sure they were dead for good.

With all the info gathered, a plan was drawn up and every team member learned their role—and that's when the scary part began. Wearing special protective armor—considerably more advanced than the forks and spoons Becks had duct-taped to her clothing when she was lost in New Jersey—teams would enter the building and methodically search everything. They always moved in pairs for safety and kept in constant contact with the team coordinators. Everyone was always on high alert during these operations, as you *never* knew where a zombie might be lurking.

For example, thinking the house was clear, one man took off his helmet and opened a kitchen cabinet over the refrigerator to look for food. To his complete shock, an emaciated female zombie launched herself out of the cabinet and locked her jaws around his mouth. By the time his fellow team members had killed her and pried open her jaws, both of his lips were hanging by mere threads of flesh.

As best as the soldiers could determine, the woman had hidden in that cabinet when the rest of her family had switched. She must also have been badly infected and switched as well, waiting for who knows how long for some poor victim to come along and open that cabinet door.

Other unnerving attacks that happened far too often came when hands or teeth reached out from under beds to grasp unsuspecting people. Team members quickly learned to reinforce the armor around their ankles and calves, as it appeared that many people—particularly children—had hidden under their beds when someone in the household had turned zombie.

20

Too terrified to come out, they died and switched there. One can only imagine what it was like to have a hand suddenly thrust out from under the bed and start clawing at your leg, or bending down to look under that bed and having a couple of zombie children lunge for your face. It wasn't long before teams had started carrying mirrors on telescoping poles to search under beds, while maintaining a healthy distance.

Basements were generally the most dreaded locations of any structures, as zombies tended to congregate in groups in their dark recesses. But even all the basement horror stories couldn't hold a candle to the account that spread fast and far about the unfortunate man who had eaten the burritos.

Early one morning, a team was clearing an apartment building in Haverstraw, New York. In one apartment, they found a box of freeze-dried burritos. One man, Jed, had missed breakfast as he had overslept, so he decided to take a quick break and reconstitute a few burritos. Even cold, they were quite tasty, especially drenched in hot sauce. Unfortunately, Jed's digestive system was not used to such heavy, spicy food, and by the time they had started clearing the top floor, Montezuma was having his revenge.

Pulling off his armor and running into a dimly lit bathroom, Jed dropped his pants, flipped up the lid of the toilet, and sat down. However, before his sphincter was able to relieve the mounting pressure, a tiny pair of teeth was sinking into his testicles. A zombie toddler had actually hidden inside the toilet bowl before he switched, and the rescuers responded to Jed's shrieking screams with a mixture of astonishment, disgust, and amusement, as the terrified man danced around the bathroom drenched in blood and burrito excrement, with the toddler dangling from his scrotum.

When Jed was fully recovered physically, he was mercifully given a desk job. Mentally, it was said he still wasn't quite right, but had started doing better once all the toilet seat lids had been removed from his housing unit.

Pete couldn't believe how normal everything looked as they drove down Main Street in Highland Falls approaching the main gate of West Point. Stores and restaurants were open, and men, women, and children went about their business as if they had never even heard the word zombie, let alone ever encountered a ravenous corpse.

The security at the main gate was tight, although the word "gate" was not quite accurate. Huge steel walls extended across the road, and only after a lengthy inspection of the vehicles, their passengers, and contents, did a section of that wall swing open to allow entry to the convoy.

One thing Pete didn't expect to see on the highly fortified military base was chickens—and not of the cowardly variety. There were literally flocks of chickens everywhere, as well as cows, goats, horses, pigs, and sheep. And wherever there used to be a grass lawn, there were now neat rows of a vegetable plants and fruit trees. Obviously, food production had become a top priority, as mankind could not survive forever on the pre-apocalypse canned food supply.

After two more checkpoints, the convoy finally stopped in front of a nondescript, three-story brick building, which could have been a 1960s school.

This is their state-of-the-art facility? Pete thought with great disappointment.

To his surprise, however, they went inside and entered an elevator that seemed to go down at least ten stories. Finally, the doors opened up on a long, central hallway lined with pairs of glass doors bearing big, bold, biohazard warnings and names of the branches of science and medicine they were researching in that particular lab—many of which had names Pete neither recognized nor understood. He caught brief glimpses of masked occupants in lab coats doing god-knows-what with equipment he had never seen before, as they passed quickly to the end of the hall to a large conference room.

At least 30 people sat squeezed around a table and dozens more stood along the walls. Everyone applauded when Pete entered, and he stopped short in amazement—not because of the applause, but because he hadn't been in a room with that many people in a very long time.

Pete was ushered to the head of the table, and only then did he remove the backpack of precious notes and data he had been willing to risk his life to deliver. From an old metal coffee can, he removed a zip lock bag filled with flash drives. Then he pulled out stacks of well-worn file folders, all overfilled with handwritten pages of notes, formulas, charts, and diagrams. His nerves and the bandages on his hands made him a bit clumsy, and one of the folders slipped from his fingers, its pages scattering across the table and floor.

"Uh, we didn't know what level of technology was left out here," Pete began, trembling slightly, as several people helped retrieve all the pieces of paper. "So, we figured that in addition to the digital files, we would go 'old school,' too."

Asking for a moment to get organized, and for glass of water, Pete was clearly intimidated by the brainpower in the room, until the colonel leaned over and whispered in his ear.

"If you can handle Devereaux, these people are a piece of cake."

Clearing his throat, twice, Pete finally began by holding up a red file folder stained with coffee rings.

"I've been told about your Eradazole, so you probably won't need our EBG files, although they are worth looking over. Our latest batch of EBG is at least effective up to ten days after infection, completely killing all eggs and larvae," Pete said nonchalantly, not realizing how impressive it was that such a small group with limited resources had developed and produced something to prevent infection after bites or exposure.

"What does EBG stand for?" someone asked.

Pete actually blushed and stammered for a moment before replying.

"Eggs-Be-Gone," he said, as the room erupted in laughter.

Pete was going to explain that it was just a silly name one of the students had given the unpronounceable compound, but he decided to minimize his embarrassment and just continue. Holding up a yellow folder, you could hear a pin drop as Pete explained Devereaux's work on the chemical cocktail he had created which inhibited the ZIPs' ability to produce a pheromone that kept zombies from attacking one another. He then surprised everyone when he said that Devereaux had abandoned that work.

Pete raised his hands when the uproar began, to quiet everyone so he could explain.

"The chemicals had to be directly injected into the zombie at various intervals over the course of two days, and then it would only have resulted in that single zombie being killed by the other zombies," he stated with the resolve that only comes with gained confidence. "However, we realized that if you could inhibit a zombie's ability to *sense* that pheromone, blocking its sense of smell, so to speak, then *it becomes a weapon against all other zombies*. And because it is still producing the pheromone, *it will not be attacked, even as it attacks others.*"

A tense stillness hung in the room as Pete slowly raised the purple folder.

"You've done it!?" Phil asked, practically bursting at the seams of his lab coat.

Pete couldn't resist a few seconds to savor the moment before he simply replied, "Yes."

The room again erupted, this time with congratulations and wild speculations about the zombie army that could be created. The colonel let the boisterous chatter continue for a minute or two before he shouted the room to order.

"Before we all conquer the world, let's hear what he has to say, shall we?" the colonel said with an air of authority not to be questioned. "Please, Mr. Hernandez, continue."

"Devereaux calls it Project Decimation, after the ancient Roman practice of killing every one in ten soldiers as punishment for a group that had deserted or mutinied. He believes that if just one in ten zombies loses its sense of smell and turns against the others, it will be sufficient to eliminate the herds."

"But *how*?" someone else asked, impatient for the facts, and just the facts.

"The key is gold nanoparticles," Pete continued, with words that made Becks' back stiffen and her eyes grow wide. "Specifically, spherical gold nanoparticle conjugates between eight to ten nanometers in size."

Pete went on to describe how tiny particles of gold had been used BZA to attach to chemotherapy drugs for highly-efficient delivery to tumors. He used terms such as "increased binding affinity," "targeting selectivity," "low immunogenic response," "long circulatory half-life," and "size-dependent receptor mediated endocytosis."

Most of the doctors understood some of what he was saying, several of the scientists in the room had a glazed look in their eyes, but all were fascinated. Throughout the entire explanation, however, Becks just grew increasingly agitated.

"Devereaux developed a compound that crippled the ZIPs' ability to sense their own pheromones, but the problem was how to get the ZIPs to absorb it. Realizing that gold nanoparticles could be just as effective with parasites as they were with cancer, he attached this compound to the nanoparticles. Injected into a zombie, they quickly and easily entered into the ZIPs and started the reaction. Within hours, these test subjects had completely lost their 'sense of smell,' and started attacking other zombies."

"Fuck me! No, *FUCK Devereaux*!" Becks finally blurted out, unable to contain herself any longer.

"*Dr. Truesdale!*" the colonel yelled, as he turned an ominous shade of crimson. "Is this your unique way of expressing your professional enthusiasm, or do you have a problem?"

Before Becks could answer, Pete turned to her with a stunned, but elated, expression.

"Truesdale!? *Rebecca* Truesdale!?" he asked, with unrestrainable excitement.

"Yes…that's me," Becks replied suspiciously as she stood up, still highly agitated. "And I am quite familiar with using gold nanoparticles against parasites because—"

"*You* wrote the paper that gave Devereaux the idea!" Pete interrupted, as even the jaw of the colonel now hung open.

Chapter 7

A lone AH-64 Apache helicopter took off from the Picatinny Arsenal. Scouting flights had recently become routine, but there was nothing routine about this helicopter, as it was bristling with Hellfire missiles and Hydra 70 rockets.

West Point had relayed a message that had caused the top brass at the arsenal to scramble a crew within minutes. As they raced to the northeast, they passed over the same suburban neighborhoods where Becks had fought for her life over the winter. Now, the spring offensive was well underway and little ribbons of smoke curled upwards across the horizon in every direction, as heavily zombie-infested structures were simply burned to the ground, rather than risk the personnel and waste the time clearing every building. They were draconian measures to be sure, but AZA, there weren't likely to be any housing shortages.

The pilot of the helicopter made a low circle at a sharp angle around a column of troops and armored vehicles advancing down the main street of a town. He didn't do it to check on their progress, but to wave to his buddies who were part of the offensive. A cheer went up from the column as they all waved back, but a flurry of small arms fire up ahead caused them all to quickly refocus and assume defensive positions.

Pulling up sharply, in case some crazy survivors started firing at them, the pilot continued on his course. Just a few minutes later the potential target was in view. The superstructure of the George Washington Bridge with its missing center span was not a pleasant sight to see, as it was a glaring and monumental reminder of all that had been lost, and just how far civilization had literally fallen. But it wasn't the snapped steel cables and crumbled concrete that made the pilot and copilot of the Apache gasp.

What at first looked like a line of ants from Manhattan slowly and inexorably invading a picnic in Fort Lee, New Jersey, resolved into a hideous conga line of zombies streaming across the makeshift bridge of debris. Enough zombies had fallen and added their bodies to the debris to create a path wide enough for the undead horde to cross three or four abreast. Horrified, the copilot immediately radioed the arsenal to report on the mass exodus. While some of the newly escaped zombies filtered off to the west and south—possibly endangering the ground troops in the spring offensive—the vast majority were heading north along the Palisades Interstate Parkway. The herd, which had to number in the hundreds of thousands, was the largest the crew had ever seen. Though it moved slowly, it would be certain to engulf anything in its path.

Instructions were given and the pilot swung into position, facing south over the Hudson River, toward the bridge. Within seconds, Hellfire missiles were indeed raining hell down the length of the makeshift pathway. Splinters of metal and wood, and chunks of concrete and burning flesh sprayed hundreds of feet into the air, as balls of fire incinerated the remaining body parts and anything combustible.

Then it was the water's turn to wreak havoc, as the partially damned river pushed hard against the weakened pathway until it finally gave way, bursting apart into the millions of small pieces from which it had been composed. Those pieces rushed passed the remnants of the bridge and started heading downriver and out to sea.

The long line of zombies waiting to escape Manhattan still pushed forward, and as impressive as the mighty explosions had been, it was an even more mesmerizing sight to see thousands and thousands of zombies being pushed from behind and dropping into the river before their forward movement finally stopped. As tempting as it was to fire on the huge crowd that now just stood there, gazing blankly over the edge, the crew decided their ordnance would be better spent on the hordes that had already crossed.

Circling around to the north, to the head of the huge sea of undead humanity, they unleashed their Hydra rockets in a lethal strafing run. A second pass created more piles of zombie hamburger meat with the 30 mm rounds from the M230 chain gun. Despite the mass destruction wrought from the Apache, however, the herd's numbers barely appeared to be touched.

With the remaining Hellfire missiles, they decided to blow enormous holes across all of the lanes of the Palisades Interstate Parkway, to at least slow down their northward progression. It would buy some precious time for the survivors who had been trying to get back on their feet in Rockland, Orange, and the surrounding counties. But even as the Apache flew away back to base, zombies stumbling into the smoldering craters in the road would eventually fill the holes and form a grisly pavement for the countless others that followed.

Chapter 8

It seemed to be a lifetime ago that Becks was a young medical student just starting out. She had been terrified at the enormity of the task that lay ahead of her, not to mention the staggering expense she would have to shoulder. Her parents offered to help, but their meager retirement income was barely sufficient to cover their property taxes, medical costs, and daily expenses.

As if it all wasn't daunting enough, she also had no small crisis in confidence. Sure, she was already a nurse, and a damn good one, but did she have what it took to be a doctor? After acing her first few classes, she slowly came to believe that she belonged, that she was just as good—if not better—than the other medical students. She could do it. She *would* do it, and nothing could derail her trip to the top of the medical field.

Then she met Dr. Martin Devereaux.

Intimidation and belittlement commenced on day one. Granted, he treated every student—and fellow faculty members—like crap, but Becks took it particularly hard. She had certainly dealt with her share of arrogant and obnoxious doctors and Ph.Ds. at the hospital and ParGenTech, but Devereaux was a special kind of sadist. He didn't attack your weaknesses to make you stronger. He targeted your strengths and ground you down.

One of young Becks' greatest strengths was her ability to think outside the established medical boxes. She looked at things differently, and always envisioned new ways of approaching illnesses and diseases. After reading about all the advances in biomedical nanoparticles, she decided to write her term paper on their possible uses against parasites to target delivery of drugs. She even thought to use nanoparticles in the body to mimic certain human cells to distract parasites away from the real cells, and thus slow their destructive progression and give more time for accompanying treatments.

Her research had been extensive and she had even made numerous trips on her few days off to the Colleges of Nanoscale Sciences and Engineering in Albany to learn as much as she could. She consulted with the best minds in the field, and conducted several highly successful experiments. In the end, her term paper resembled more of a doctoral thesis, and Becks fully expected to receive high praise and honors.

Instead, Devereaux gave her a C with no word of explanation.

"This has to be a mistake," an incredulous Becks told her friends at school when they picked up their papers from Devereaux's assistant.

When she later went to his office to ask about the poor grade, she still fully expected he would apologize at the obvious error and give her a glowing A+.

"I don't know who *you* think you are," Devereaux barked at Becks with contempt, "but *I* know who *I* am, and that's the grade *I* say this paper deserves."

For the first time in her life, mild-mannered Rebecca Truesdale went ballistic. Students and teachers within earshot of the ensuing argument stopped to listen in wonder and admiration that someone had the guts to stand up to the mighty Devereaux, but it was all for naught. For every sound argument Becks presented—albeit red-faced and yelling—Devereaux obstinately countered that *he* was the expert and if she didn't like the grade of C, he would gladly change it to an F and recommend her for expulsion.

Becks had no recourse. Devereaux was far too famous and influential for her to garner any support against him, and he brought in far too much money for the university to even consider taking any type of disciplinary action. Becks was told she was free to file a complaint, but it would not go well with her plans of someday graduating from that institution.

The young medical student was devastated, and the rising star on campus sank below the radar. She still did well on all her other courses, but the blazing fire within her had been extinguished.

In a strange twist of fate, it would take a zombie apocalypse to reignite that flame and motivate her to reach her true potential. And now that she was a highly respected doctor and researcher, at the top of who was left in her field, Devereaux had to rear his ugly, hateful head, with an idea that had been sparked by the very paper he had so harshly criticized.

"Dr. Truesdale," the colonel began after Becks had related to everyone in the conference room the condensed story of her research, the disputed paper, and the battle with Devereaux. "You are the obvious choice to accompany Mr. Hernandez back to Columbia to speak to Dr. Devereaux, and extract him, if possible. I trust your personal issues will not prevent you from helping to save the human race?"

"For god's sake, Becks, say something!" Phil whispered, as he elbowed her in the ribs when she didn't reply right away.

"I'm thinking about it," she whispered back, her blood still boiling.

Before she could speak up and respond, however, a sergeant rushed into the room and handed the colonel a flash drive. While he didn't speak a word, and only gave the colonel a stilted nod, his expression spoke volumes, and a chill swept through everyone in the room.

"It appears that your information was unfortunately accurate," the colonel said to Pete, as he stuck the flash drive into the side of the huge screen in the front of the conference room. He signaled for the lights to be turned off, and then the video footage from the Apache helicopter began.

Gasps, choked sobs, and cries of shock and horror arose from the dark room. No words could adequately express what they were seeing, or what they were all feeling. A tidal wave of death was heading their way, and as things were, survivors would not be able to stand up against it. They would have to run, or die.

When the lights came back on, Becks stood up. The anger that had burned so hotly just moments ago had chilled to an icy fear, and a stone-cold resolve.

"I'll be ready to go see Devereaux within the hour."

"Like hell you're going without me," Cam said, strapping on his holsters.

Word of Sticky Pete's arrival and the massive zombie herd had spread like wildfire throughout West Point, and Cam was already gearing up when Becks entered their quarters.

"Unnecessary," Becks replied. "Quick in and out. Simple."

"Nothing was ever simple *before* the zombie apocalypse, and it sure as hell is never simple *now*," Cam added with emphasis. "Just try and keep me from going."

Cam certainly had a point, but the mission *should* be quick and easy, and she really didn't need a body guard. On the other hand, she was trembling ever so slightly at the thought of going back "out there." Since being rescued from the hell of New Jersey, she had not left the confines of West Point. She would probably be fine on her own once the mission got underway, but it certainly would be nice to have Cam by her side—not that she would admit to it.

"Suit yourself," Becks simply said, as she stripped off her lab clothes and donned her beloved camo clothing, boots, and a host of pistols and knives.

It would have been helpful if they could have had at least a few hours to more thoroughly go through all of the Project Decimation data, but from Pete's description of Devereaux's condition, every minute counted. A civilian cardiac surgeon would also be accompanying them—the same man who Becks had first met when she opened the clinic on Bannerman's Island, which now seemed like it had been decades ago.

A young Army doctor would also be going, as, after Becks, he seemed to have the most knowledge of biomedical nanoparticles. The team was rounded out by two heavily-armed Rangers, each a mountain of muscles who had gained reputations for being one man armies. Still, Becks would take Cam any day in a fight, but she hoped that this mission would not require any violence—and that included what she wanted to do to Devereaux.

They were all driven to the parade grounds where the transport helicopter awaited them. Pete looked sweaty and anxious, but otherwise alert, no doubt as the result of some potent amphetamines to keep him on his feet. What he really needed was about twelve hours of uninterrupted sleep, but the clock was ticking, and as Becks had once said, there would be plenty of time to sleep once you've turned zombie.

The young Army doctor, Julian Ritter, clutched hard to a stack of papers and shut his eyes when the helicopter lifted briskly up from the ground. He clearly didn't like to fly, and Becks also suspected that he had never been beyond the gates of West Point since the apocalypse began. To distract him, she asked him if those papers contained the questions the medical staff had for Devereaux.

"Huh? Yeah, I mean, yes, Ma'am. Uh, these are the questions," Julian replied, rubbing his forehead repeatedly. "Uh, sorry, Ma'am. I, uh, I've never been in a helicopter before. And to tell the truth, I, uh, don't get out much. Like *never*."

"It will all be just fine," Cam said in his smooth, reassuring tone, as he patted the young man on the shoulder. "Just stay close and listen to instructions, and it will all be okay."

Julian relaxed his death grip on the stack of papers and he and Becks began discussing the various questions and comments the medical staff

31

had hastily scribbled down. She was pleased at the young doctor's knowledge of nanoparticles, and it was clear he had kept up with the latest research right up until the apocalypse began. He knew things that Becks didn't, but he had never actually conducted any experiments, and only had a basic knowledge of parasites.

They were both so absorbed in their discussion they didn't realize they were hovering over Columbia University until they heard the pilot shout to Pete for the location of Devereaux's building. Unfortunately, that building had a roof covered in solar panels, rainwater collection tanks and pipes, and buckets and containers of all shapes and sizes filled with vegetable plants.

"I'll have to land over there," the pilot said, pointing to another structure about 100 yards away.

The roof of that building had a couple of large air conditioning units, but there would be just enough room to set down safely—if it was strong enough to hold the big helicopter.

"That one's not secure," Pete shouted back over the roar of the engines.

"Oh boy, here we go," Cam said under his breath, not intending anyone else to hear, as he surreptitiously gripped both pistols.

There was a brief discussion between the crew members and Pete, and it was decided it would be safer to drop everyone down to the roof of the secure building, than land on the other structure and then possibly have to fight their way down several flights of zombie-infested stairways, and cross 100 yards of open ground. No one disagreed, although Julian suspected he would throw up or wet himself either way.

Harnesses were distributed, and as a side door slid open and a crew member began to explain how to safely lower yourself down the rope, Julian did indeed drop to his knees and vomit. Fortunately, he did it with his head stuck outside the door so none of it got in the aircraft, but the pilot did have to adjust his position so no one would have to drop feet first onto the splattered half-digested scrambled eggs and bacon below.

BZA, Cam had taken Becks zip lining, and she had loved the sense of freedom flying through the air. This was much shorter and straight down, but she still felt like a Navy Seal storming a terrorist compound as she rapidly descended to the roof—although it was a fantasy she wisely did not share in the presence of two *Army* Rangers.

Everyone landed safely—and all of them tried to pretend not to notice Julian screaming like a little girl the entire way down. The helicopter then moved off and slowly and carefully settled down on top of the other building, where it would wait until they had gathered all the info they needed, and perhaps Devereaux himself.

Pete's first act when he landed on the roof was to rush over to the row of potted tomato plants that had been blown over by the rotors' strong downdraft. Even though he would be leaving again—probably never to return—they had all lavished so much tender loving care on their rooftop garden he was compelled to stand the plants upright and gently brush off the dirt from their leaves.

As he was clearing off the last plant, the door to the roof swung open and Becks and company all drew their weapons. But it was just Max and Arjun, who rushed toward Pete with wild exuberance. The two men were pretty banged up, but they were otherwise okay, and it was a very happy reunion as his two friends congratulated Pete and said they knew he could make it. The mood instantly shifted, however, when Pete asked about the others, especially Erin. Max and Arjun suddenly took a step back and fell silent. They didn't need to actually say it, but Pete needed to know how it had happened.

There had been a terrible struggle down by the river after they had launched Pete on the raft. Hundreds of zombies just seemed to come out of nowhere. Jiang had been grabbed and taken down by about a dozen of them, and Josh was also overwhelmed. Erin had rushed to their defense and was able to save both of them, and while the two men had been badly bitten, they would survive.

Erin, however, had been bitten in both wrists, severing arteries. She tried to run back with them, but just a block away from safety, she collapsed and died in the street, despite their best efforts to staunch the flow of blood. Pete staggered backwards at the news, and Max and Arjun each grabbed a shoulder to help keep him upright. Pete had really liked Erin, maybe even loved her, but even in the apocalypse he never found the courage to tell her.

There was more bad news, too. Back near the river, Margo had climbed a tree to pick off zombies at long range to clear the path ahead of the retreating team. Max had insisted they all stick together, but there was

33

no reasoning with the pigheaded woman. Margo said she would be right behind them, but they never saw her again.

Everyone just stood there silently to give Pete a moment, but a distant groan of hunger rising up from the gathering crowd of zombies below in the courtyard snapped Pete back into focus. He was now more determined than ever to initiate Project Decimation.

Chapter 9

The acrid stench of burned flesh still hung in the air from the Apache helicopter's attack on the zombies crossing the makeshift bridge, as well as the multitudes that had made it to New Jersey. A gust of wind from that direction sent the foul odor towards Columbia University, but while everyone smelled it, no one commented, and they were all just happy to get inside and let the heavy metal door slam shut behind them.

As they descended the stairs, Becks was half hoping that Devereaux would be dead already, but she was not to be so lucky. Sticky Pete entered the lab first and all of the other students rushed to see him, except for Jiang and Josh who were recuperating from their wounds in the medical bay, as they had named their improvised infirmary. Pete introduced everyone in his group, and Becks did the same for the members of her team.

"Where is he?" the cardiac surgeon asked once the greetings and formalities had been dispensed.

"I'll take you to him," Arjun said somberly. "He's not breathing well."

Becks and Julian went with the others to start going over the apparatus they used to produce gold nanoparticles. Cam and the Rangers stood by and listened to a lot of words and terms they didn't understand, such as "reduction of aqueous chloroauric acid by citrate." It was at times like this that Cam realized just how big the divide was between him and Becks, but it was also at these moments that he was proudest of her...and loved her the most.

Cam understood very little about the ZIPs pheromones, how the zombies sensed them, and why they had to go to such lengths to create these nano things to block some sort of receptors. He was tempted to suggest just sticking cotton balls up a zombie's nose—or simply cutting off its nose—to keep it from smelling these pheromones, but he knew enough to realize that if it was that easy, Becks or one of the other braniacs would have done it long ago. Indeed, it was far more complicated than that, as the network of ZIPs throughout the body had pheromone receptors in all mucous membranes, as well as certain parts of the skin.

Cam was also impressed that after being in isolation for so long, none of the Columbia students initially had any questions about what was going on in the outside world. Their only focus was to explain every detail of their research and experimental successes, as well as their failures. One of the Rangers finally interrupted to remind all the eggheads that they were going to be evacuated and should start packing as much of the equipment, chemicals, and data they needed. You would have thought they were a bunch of kindergartners let out of school for Christmas vacation by the level of enthusiasm and energy that ensued.

Arjun and the cardiac surgeon returned with grim expressions. The other Ranger asked for a "sit rep" on Devereaux.

"I don't know what has kept him alive this long," the surgeon replied, "except that he is one stubborn old bastard. His heart and kidneys are failing, and his liver is probably shot. If he lasts the night, I will be surprised. There's no way he can be moved."

"I'll let headquarters know the news," the Ranger said, reaching for his radio.

"He wants to see you," the surgeon said turning to where Becks and Julian were standing, but when both of them started for the door with Arjun, the surgeon added, "No, just you Becks."

Taking a deep breath, Becks glanced over at Cam, who shot her a "you had better behave" look. This was a moment she had been dreading since she heard Devereaux was still alive, and despite all of her academic accomplishments and acts of bravery in the field, not to mention the incredible grit it took to survive on her own throughout the winter, at that particular instant she felt like a shy and inept freshman student. Devereaux was already pushing her buttons and she hadn't even seen him yet.

Walking down a long hall, they approached a small lab that had been turned into an office/bedroom. An unpleasant odor wafted out of the door, one that Becks had smelled many times in the hospital—the smell of impending death. Just a few years ago, Devereaux was a vibrant terror of a man; not exactly a picture of good health, but certainly one of considerable vitality and energy. Becks was not prepared for that pale, frail, ghost of a human being that now sat hunched in a wheelchair with IVs dripping into both withered arms. She never would have recognized him.

"Dr. Devereaux?" she asked, almost in a whisper as she stopped short in the doorway.

"*Miss*…Truesdale," he emphasized between labored breaths.

Sympathy vanished as Becks felt her blood pressure skyrocket at the obvious slight. She had been the first to recover from infection, thanks to medication she helped develop. In recognition for her heroic fight and contribution to a drug that would save countless lives, the university had subsequently bestowed upon her a medical degree, which she had more than earned, and was only one class shy of completing anyway. The story had not only been big news locally, but internationally, as well. There was no way Devereaux had not heard about her work and medical degree.

"That's *Doctor* Truesdale, actually," she replied, trying not to clench her teeth too hard.

"Oh yes…I do recall some publicity stunt…to make you an *honorary* doctor," Devereaux replied with the same level of contempt he had always exhibited toward her.

This time, she would not stand for it, death bed or not.

"If you plan on being the same obnoxious asshole as the last time we met, then I'm going to leave right now," Becks said in a low and dangerous tone that even made Arjun's skin crawl.

"And if you plan…on being the same egotistical…immature…bitch that you were, you might as well…leave right now," Devereaux responded, straightening all the aching and brittle mean bones in his body to look as formidable as a dying man could.

"*Egotistical!? Immature!?*" Becks shouted, barely able to restrain herself from ringing his scrawny neck.

"You heard me! If you had just listened…to what I was trying to tell you…about the flaws in your methodology…and imprecise conclusions. But no…you took my criticism personally…and you gave up…abandoned the research."

Becks mind was reeling. Was this just more of his cruel tricks and mind games, or had she let her ego blind her?

"So, that was all *my* fault?" she said in a more subdued tone, but still dripping with a heavy dose of anger.

"You think academia is all shiny gold stars…and cupcakes at recess?" he continued, as his breathing seemed to improve and his voice grew louder. "Do you think the medical profession or the pharmaceutical industry wouldn't have chewed you up and spit you out at that point in your life?"

"Well…maybe if you had *helped* me. Maybe if you had *one word* of encouragement," Becks said, almost in a whisper, sinking rapidly back into self-doubt.

"What the hell did you expect from me?" Devereaux replied, in what almost seemed like a civil tone. "The last thing an old scientist wants to see is some brilliant young student still wet behind the ears coming up with an idea he didn't think of himself."

Becks had *never* considered jealousy as part of his motive. Between that alien concept and his use of the term "brilliant," she didn't know what to think now. Before she could respond, however, the surgeon, Cam, and a few of the students rushed into the room. She hadn't noticed that Arjun had run to get help when they started shouting at each other.

"Becks, what the hell is wrong with you?" the surgeon yelled as he took Devereaux's pulse and then put the stethoscope to his chest. "Are you *trying* to kill him?"

"Get your goddamn hands off me," Devereaux growled, pushing the surgeon away as best he could. "I haven't felt this good in months. *Miss* Truesdale and I were just recalling the good old days."

Both Cam and the cardiologist gave Becks stern looks, but decided to let it go so as not to escalate the situation and aggravate Devereaux any further. It was also decided that Becks and Julian would spend as much time as they could with Devereaux, learning as much as possible about his ZIPs research.

"But first," Devereaux said, with something of a rare smile, "you all need to see Jaws."

For a moment, there was some doubt about Devereaux's sanity. Did he actually want everyone to watch a shark movie?

"Jaws is our most unique test subject," Max offered, seeing the confused looks on everyone's faces. "They are all in the basement. I'll take you to them."

Max and Arjun led Becks and her team down several flights of stairs to an expansive basement which had a strange wall with several reinforced doors and many small windows. Max started a generator and then Arjun flipped on a bank of switches after Max signaled him. Everyone was momentarily startled when the sudden light revealed hideous zombie faces pressed against many of the windows. Julian had to suppress his urge to run.

Beckoning everyone to a larger, central window, Max explained that they had welded together these rebar pens, and one of the engineering students had hooked up a control panel and wires so that everything could be handled remotely. He said that the ten zombies in the pens on the left had been injected with the gold nanoparticle serum. The two dozen zombies in the pens on the right had not been treated. But there was one pen in the center of the room that held someone special. Banging on the window and shouting to rile up its occupant, the six-foot-five-inch, 250 pounds of muscular zombie within grabbed the bars of his cage and growled in hunger.

"Behold, Jaws!" Max said with great pride, albeit a somewhat twisted pride—like Dr. Frankenstein showing his creature to the world.

"Ho-ly shit!" one of the Rangers exclaimed, which were the exact words on the tips of everyone's tongues.

"I can't take credit for the hands, but the teeth are all mine," the former dental student said, beaming.

As the massive zombie growled, he revealed rows of razor-sharp, pointed, stainless steel teeth that Max had designed and bonded to the zombie's real teeth. On the tips of his fingers were fierce-looking claws.

"Human teeth really aren't the most efficient for tearing into flesh," Max continued. "So what better animal to emulate than the shark, with its rows of deadly teeth. Of course, the real trick was to design them in a way that Jaws didn't cut his own mouth to ribbons. And as for the razor claws on his hands, Erin had made those using heavy duty work gloves and scalpels."

"*Why the hell* would anyone make a zombie even more dangerous?" the cardiologist asked, completely dumbfounded and horrified.

This time Arjun spoke up, and was clearly surprised that anyone would need to ask that question.

"If you are creating a team of zombie 'special forces,' don't you want to equip them with the deadliest weapons? I mean, it's not like we could give them guns. But let us show you, as a demonstration is worth a thousand words."

Arjun turned a switch, which spun a gear that pulled a wire to open a door latch of one of the pens on the right. A female zombie in her forties staggered out and headed straight for the large viewing window. Julian jumped back as it pressed its half-decomposed face against the glass, trying to get to a meal.

Max then released the door lock to Jaws' pen, but he didn't step out right away. What Becks' team hadn't noticed before, was that Jaws was wearing a harness attached to a heavy steel cable. Only after Max started turning a dial did Jaws get enough slack in the line to leave his pen—and make a beeline for the female zombie at the viewing window. The ensuing scene was so brutal—bloodier than a school of piranhas shredding a rodent—no one could continue to watch it to the end, but it gave them hope, as they had never dared to hope since the start of the apocalypse.

Instead of just two powerful hands grabbing the female zombie's arms, the scalpel-tipped fingers plunged deep into her flesh, slicing her biceps, triceps, and blood vessels. Then Jaws opened his mouth revealing his shiny, new, metal teeth, which he promptly sank into the female's throat. Clenching down hard, he tore it out a huge chunk of meat, as arterial blood sprayed all over the viewing window. The female zombie dropped to the floor like a rock, and after swallowing his appetizer, Jaws bent down to start the main course. It was at this point that everyone had to turn away.

"I guess you've all gotten the point," Max said, slightly ashamed that he took such joy at his creation eviscerating a human body, even if it was a zombie human body.

As Max reached for the dial to reel Jaws back into his cage, one of the Rangers clamped his beefy hand down to stop him.

"Let him eat his fill," the Ranger said. "It will make him easier to transport."

"*Say what?*" Julian asked, not looking forward to sharing a seat on the helicopter with Jaws.

"I'll check with HQ, but I'm fairly certain they are going to want all of these test subjects injected with the serum," he explained, and then looked to Becks for her input.

"It would certainly give us a big head start on the project," she had to admit. "In fact, getting them to West Point should be a priority."

By the time they had gone back upstairs, the orders had already come through to secure the Project Decimation zombies and transport them to West Point immediately. As it was getting dark, it was also decided to keep Becks and her team at Columbia overnight, because there wasn't enough room for everyone on a single flight. No one was thrilled with the idea, but it made the most sense.

"Simple in and out, huh?" Cam said sarcastically to Becks, but then changed his tone. "You gonna be okay spending the night here?"

Becks didn't want to admit the sick feeling in the pit of her stomach at the prospect of her first night outside the protective walls of West Point since her ordeal in New Jersey, so she just did what any woman would—smiled and lied.

"I'll be fine. I'll be working with Devereaux all night so I will lose all concept of time and place. You know me."

"Yeah, I know you," Cam said with a wink. "Able to lie through a charming smile."

"I'm more worried about you," Becks said, quickly changing the subject. "You have to help get those zombies on the helicopter."

"These students know what they're doing ... I hope," he said, as he gave her a light kiss on the cheek as he left her to her work. He then headed back down to the basement.

Becks was used to Devereaux's clipped sentences and rapid-fire way of making his points, and she truly felt like a student again trying to keep pace and take notes. Julian, however, had no idea what to expect and did the unforgivable—he interrupted Devereaux, twice, to ask him to slow down and give fuller explanations. His illness and limited energy made Devereaux ignore the first interruption, but the second was too much to bear.

"Young man," Devereaux began, summoning all the venom he had left, "In a few hours I'll be dead and gone, but you're still going to be stupid if you don't pay attention!"

Becks would never admit it, but she was relieved to have someone else there to take the brunt of Devereaux's ire. And so the three worked late into the night scribbling notes and making audio recordings of every word of wisdom and piece of knowledge Devereaux had the strength to divulge. They had to take frequent breaks for the dying man to rest and receive attention from the cardiologist, but after every break, Devereaux had more labored breathing, seemed less focused, and most telltale of all, was less combative and cruel.

Meanwhile in the basement, several students, Cam, and the Rangers were dressed in full biohazard gear and moving quickly to prepare the undead test subjects for transport. Using one of Erin's homemade stun rods, they would temporarily render the zombie unconscious. It would then be gagged, dressed in a biohazard suit to prevent spreading infection, and then its legs were lashed together and its hands were bound tightly behind its back.

Jaws was a little more work, as he required a special Hannibal Lecter-type mask. They also removed his claw gloves. It wasn't easy jamming his enormous body into a biohazard suit, which was clearly not an extra-large size. They also made sure to double up on the hand and leg restraints.

It was also a lot of work making sure none of the zombies would be able to get loose during transport, but that part was nothing compared to carrying them up all those flights of stairs. Devereaux had naturally insisted that his zombie soldiers be the tallest and strongest physical specimens they could capture, which of course, made sense.

The two Rangers carried one zombie up the stairs by themselves, but it took three students and Cam to handle one. By the fourth and fifth trips, however, everyone was exhausted and winded, and it took all six of them to drag, carry, and maneuver Jaws up the long staircases and out to the roof. Once all of the test subjects were gathered, the helicopter hovered overhead while each zombie was attached to the cable and hoisted aboard.

The pilot was not a happy camper. Even though they were all securely tied, he insisted that the zombies be placed in a big cargo net which was closed with steel clips and then strapped to the deck of the helicopter. One of the Rangers agreed to ride along to keep an extra set of eyes on the bizarre squirming and groaning cargo, which lifted off into the darkness, passing over the huge herd below that continued to inch its way northward.

By 3am, only Becks and Devereaux were still awake. Even Julian had fallen asleep, face-first onto his stack of notes.

"Enough, enough," Devereaux finally said, as Becks had continued to pepper him with questions. "I can't...tell you *every* thing I...know. You...know enough...to...make Project Decimation...a success."

"Should I get the doctor?" Becks asked, referring to the cardiologist.

"You're...*supposed* to be a doctor. What do...you think?" he said with his unique brand of sarcasm.

"I think," she said, pausing for a moment, "we might as well let the doctor sleep. And I just want to thank you for sharing all this incredible knowledge with –"

"Oh… shut the hell…up!" Devereaux said in true, nasty Devereaux style. "Don't …start kissing…my ass now…just because…I'm dying. Just make…this work…and save…the fucking world…god damn it."

Becks felt herself getting angry again. It took a lot for her to try to say something nice, and he just threw it back in her face. Before she could respond however, Devereaux's long, rasping exhale was not followed by a labored inhale. She waited a few moments and then searched his neck for a pulse. She then ran her hand over his eyes to close them, and pulled a sheet off the bed to cover him. Then she curled up on that bed and fell fast asleep.

I'll need every minute of rest I can get, she thought before drifting off. *Because starting tomorrow, saving the fucking world will be on my shoulders, god damn it…*

Chapter 10

The day dawned with red, ominous clouds traversing the eastern horizon, which soon began to spread and thicken to a decidedly dark gray gloom. Thunderstorms and high winds moved up the coast so the helicopter fleet at West Point was grounded until the weather improved. AZA, every plane and helicopter was precious, and essentially irreplaceable, and not to be risked unless it was an absolute emergency.

News of Devereaux's death brought an even more somber mood, and Becks was surprised to see that tears were actually being shed. Sticky Pete said something about preparing the body and carrying out Devereaux's last wishes, and asked that Becks and her team be on the roof in an hour for a brief service.

Death was so prevalent AZA that funeral services were a luxury in which few survivors could indulge. Becks was not looking forward to any emotional and sentimental bullshit about a man she detested, but she would stand out in the rain with the others, at least as a show of respect for a scientist whose efforts just might save the human race—although why it had to be on the roof, she couldn't begin to imagine, unless he wanted to be buried in their vegetable garden?

A carton of those cheap, disposable slickers was passed around, which did nothing to prevent the wind-driven rain from pelting the faces of the funeral party as they filed out onto the roof. Devereaux's body was already there—naked and strapped to a piece of plywood!

"What the..." Cam whispered to Becks, who was equally dumbfounded and just shrugged her shoulders and shook her head in disbelief. Jagged bolts of lightning flashed across the sky and thunder exploded like artillery shells as the living formed a circle around Devereaux's withered, nude corpse. Becks was trying not to look at the unpleasant sight, but she noticed some odd, discolored areas of swelling in his arms, legs, and torso, almost as if some type of liquid had been injected under the skin. If it was an attempt at embalming, it was the worst job she had ever seen.

"Dr. Martin Devereaux was not an easy man to like," Sticky Pete began, shouting to be heard over the rumbles of thunder.

Amen to that, Becks thought.

"But he was an intellectual force to be reckoned with, and respected," Pete continued. "Even in death, he insisted on continuing his research. He asked that his body be injected with a new infectious agent he had developed."

At this point, all the members of Becks' team took a step back from the body, both alarmed and puzzled.

"It is only deadly to the ZIPs," Pete added quickly before continuing. "From the start of the apocalypse, Dr. Devereaux's sole focus was on finding ways to prevent infections and kill the ZIPs. Perhaps if Project Decimation is successful, and civilization returns to the earth, statues of him will be erected to his genius."

Hopefully, those statues won't be naked, Becks thought, putting a hand to her face to conceal a smile.

"Today, we honor the man by granting his last wish—to feed his infected corpse to the zombies he swore to destroy."

A sharp clap of thunder punctuated the unique eulogy, and Max, Arjun, and another male student joined Pete in grabbing the broomstick handles of the plywood stretcher. They carried the body to the edge of the roof, where another student used a knife to cut the straps. That student then brought a trumpet to his lips and attempted to play *Taps*, but fortunately, the thunder drowned out the many sour notes.

Then slowly, ever so slowly, the piece of plywood was tilted until Devereaux's corpse slid off. It impacted the pavement below with a skull-shattering and bone-splintering force, and within seconds the crowd of zombies was tearing into the flesh and brains of one of the most brilliant humans to ever live.

Everyone was silent as they descended the stairs back to the labs. Towels were passed around and minutes continued to tick by without anyone speaking. What *could* one say of such a thing? The silence was finally broken by the crackle of a garbled and staticky message coming over the remaining Ranger's radio. The second sentence was heard clearly after the Ranger moved to the window.

"Columbia One, this is WPHQ, do you read me? Over."

Becks couldn't hear what else was being said over the radio as everyone had suddenly started talking at once, now that the tension had been broken. The students were all abuzz about finally leaving Manhattan—something many of them never thought they would live to see—and they asked all kinds of questions about the food at West Point, the hot showers, the labs, and then more questions about the food. After a couple of minutes, Becks heard her name being called over the din.

"Dr. Truesdale," the Ranger with the radio was shouting, "Dr. Masterson needs to speak with you."

Becks assumed that Phil wanted to talk about the cargo of zombies, and she had some information for him she had gotten from Devereaux that she wanted to share, as well. Becks made her way through the pack of excited students to get to the Ranger by the window, where the radio reception was better.

"Hey, Phil, it's Becks. Don't say I never gave you anything. Over," she said, thinking she was making a joke about the delivery of the bound and gagged zombies. But Phil was not laughing.

"Becks, uh, I hate to ask this," he began, pausing the transmission for a moment. "But we've been going over all of Devereaux's notes and the equipment you sent, and, well, for the scale of production we want, we need better apparatus for making the gold nanoparticle serum. Over."

"OK, I'll ask the students, but I think they packed up everything they had. Over," Becks replied, puzzled, and oddly troubled by Phil's tone.

"Yeah, Becks, that's just it," Phil said, clearly uncomfortable with what needed to be said, "That equipment is fine to produce enough serum for a dozen zombie soldiers, but we need hundreds, or better yet, thousands. Over."

"Spit it out, Phil. What are you getting at? Over."

"We believe we can really scale up production with the equipment they have up in Albany, at the College of Nanoscale Science," Phil finally said, as if blurting out a confession, but not the entire confession.

"Sounds good to me. They have—well had—state-of-the-art stuff. Just make sure that whoever is going to pick it up knows what they're doing," Becks said, and then realized she was the one best qualified for the mission. "Oh. You want me to go, don't you?"

"It's not that *I want* you to go," Phil said with emphasis, and guilt. "But we've all been talking—been up all night, in fact—and with your experience and knowledge, we've realized you are the obvious choice. No one else here has *any* experience with nanoparticles. But we all get it if you don't want to go, after all you've been through. Over."

46

Becks' heart was beating a little faster, and beads of sweat had begun to form on her brow. She knew that while some of the capital was secure, Albany was still considered a frontier town, with a large population of zombies still roaming the streets, not to mention filling many of the buildings.

When the spring offensive began in northern New Jersey, troops had been pulled from many of the locations in the Hudson Valley, including Albany, where to her knowledge the secure perimeter was being maintained, but not expanded. She doubted that a school of nano science was high on the list of places that needed to be cleared. Until now.

"How bad is it up there?" Becks asked calmly, despite the anxiety creeping up her spine.

"It's in the Red Zone," Phil replied, as if telling a friend she had a terrible disease. "We are trying to get more intel, but as of now, we honestly have no idea what conditions are like inside the buildings, or on the roads leading from the secure zone. And they don't have more than a handful of soldiers to spare. But we could just tell Julian to go. No one will blame you if you're not up to it."

"He is completely useless under pressure," Becks said in a softer tone, just to be sure she was not overheard by anyone in the lab—not that it was a secret, even to Julian. "I'm not about to wimp out when a massive herd has just been unleashed. The weather still sucks here, so how soon can you get a chopper to pick us up?"

The radio was silent for a few moments, which made Becks' blood run even colder.

"Uh, that's the other thing," Phil replied sheepishly. "Doesn't look like the storms will move out anytime soon, and every minute counts. They've sent a boat to pick you up, but you'll have to make your way down to the river, which from what Pete said, will not be easy."

Becks gave the radio back to the Ranger so he could talk to HQ about the details of where and when the boat would be arriving. She found Sticky Pete and quietly said something in his ear, making his eyes widen, and then he hurried over to the Ranger to offer his knowledge of the best pickup location. Then Becks found Cam, and he instantly knew something was wrong.

"It just got a whole lot less simple, didn't it?" he asked, resigned to more trouble.

Chapter 11

The craters in the Palisades Interstate Parkway left by the Apache's rockets were rapidly becoming ponds in the relentless downpours. The herd of zombies continued marching inexorably forward, nonetheless, completely ignorant of the treacherous terrain that lay ahead. Pushed from behind, the zombies along the leading edge of the herd fell in to the craters.

As those soulless bodies struggled in the water and mud, another row of zombies fell on top of them, and so on, and so on, eventually crushing, drowning, and suffocating those at the bottom of the piles. It would take a while, but body by body of men, women, and children, those craters would fill up to street level. Then it would be the countless feet of the herd staggering over the fallen that would compact those bodies even further.

Any zombie who stopped to try to feed on the corpses of the fallen was also trampled to death, but with time, all edible flesh at the surface of this gruesome pavement would be consumed, and the herd would continue over the bones of the dead as if the craters never existed.

West Point was buzzing with activity. While the military minds planned defensive strategies to protect the Hudson Valley, every scientist, doctor, and lab tech was working feverishly on Project Decimation. One young cadet, Lionel Winston, who had been volunteering in the lab during his free time, was asked by Phil to take up a collection of gold jewelry, as they would need it to make the chloroauric acid for the gold nanoparticle production.

"No gold-filled crap, Lionel," Phil explained. "Fourteen karat at least, but eighteen karat is better. Here, start with this."

Phil removed his own wedding ring as if it physically hurt to do so, but he couldn't let his emotions prevent this important work.

"Yes, sir, Dr. Masterson," Lionel replied, but hesitated to begin his mission.

"Is there a problem?" Phil asked. "Perhaps you don't understand the gravity of the situation?"

"Yes, sir, Doctor, I most certainly do," Lionel responded crisply. "But it may not be necessary to collect jewelry. Wouldn't 24 karat gold be ideal?"

Phil had to laugh before he spoke. "Yes, son, that would be most ideal, but I'm afraid I'm fresh out of gold bullion. You wouldn't happen to have a few bars to spare, would you?"

"Yes, sir, I do," Lionel said, and recognized that Phil was in no mood for a joke, so he quickly added, "Well, not me personally, sir. The West Point Mint has stacks and stacks of gold bars. Second only to Fort Knox, or so I heard."

Phil stared at the young man for a moment to make sure he was serious, and then grabbed his wedding ring and shoved it back on his finger as fast as he could. He then scribbled a note and handed it to the young man.

"You take this note to General Bridges, ASAP, and tell him to do whatever he has to, to get into that vault."

"Yes, sir, Dr. Masterson!"

Lionel Winston promptly sprinted out of the lab, and didn't stop running until he found the general and presented Phil's note.

"You know I'm going to verify this request with Dr. Masterson, and what will happen to you if he didn't write this note?" the general said, eyeing the cadet suspiciously.

"Yes, sir, General. Please confirm immediately."

The general's assistant did just that, but much to Lionel's dismay, he was then dismissed. The gold would be delivered to the lab by the appropriate personnel and guards, and he would not be allowed to set eyes on a treasure beyond his wildest dreams. But at least the gold did exist, and it just might help combat this wildest of nightmares, which with every passing minute was inching closer to West Point.

Chapter 12

"Froot Loops are a terrible thing to waste," Becks said, trying to lighten the mood.

She had just informed Julian that they were going to have to travel through zombie-infested streets to get to the river, where a boat would take them to Albany, where they would then be entering the Red Zone. For a second or two, Julian took on the hue of the lime Froot Loops he had just eaten for breakfast. He then proceeded to throw up the multicolored breakfast cereal all over his shoes. It would have been kind of pretty, if it hadn't been vomit.

"You know, you can always opt out," Becks added, feeling a little sorry for him, but also feeling a bit of contempt.

After all, Julian was a soldier, even though the only reason he had enlisted was to get a free medical degree. He thought he might be posted stateside to Walter Reed Medical Center in Bethesda, or at the worst, the military hospital in Ramstein, Germany. Of course, no one thought the worst that could happen was zombies, but still, he wore the uniform so he should do his duty.

But will I be able to do my duty? Becks wondered, as they geared up for their trip down to the river. There was a steady current of anxiety running through her—a constant thrumming that resonated with every rapid heartbeat throughout her network of jangled nerves.

"If I freeze, smack me. *Hard,*" Becks whispered to Cam, as they strapped on some body armor that Erin had made from sheet metal and Velcro to protect their ankles and forearms. Too bad Erin hadn't also made wrist guards, otherwise she might still be alive. With that in mind, Sticky Pete urged everyone to wrap a few pieces of duct tape around their wrists, which everyone, including the Ranger, did.

Their team consisted of the Ranger, Cam, Julian, Becks, Pete, Max, and a short, slightly overweight, middle-aged woman named Martha, with limp, white-streaked, mousy brown hair. Neither Cam nor Becks had noticed her before now, but then that was the story of her life. She had been a lab assistant at Columbia for many years and her nondescript appearance and low key (or was it no key?) personality caused her to blend in with the lab instruments and furniture so thoroughly that coworkers often forgot she was in the same room. Some even forgot she worked there.

Cam discreetly questioned Sticky Pete about bringing Martha along on what promised to be a strenuous and dangerous mission. Pete explained that she had a good knowledge of nanoparticles and had worked closely with Devereaux, so she was definitely someone they wanted to help choose the right equipment and supplies.

"Plus, we think she's going through menopause and I pity the zombie who tries to mess with her!" Pete concluded with a wink.

Pete held a mission briefing with a hastily drawn map made with a black Sharpie on a big piece of cardboard. He traced the prior route they had taken with the raft to get to the river, but added that they would probably have to go even farther north this time as the situation had gotten much worse. Then Max used a red Sharpie to highlight the areas where they had encountered the most zombies. He hesitated and got a little choked up as he included the location where Erin had received her fatal wounds, and everyone gave him a moment before he continued.

Diversionary spheres were thrown from the roof of the building in the opposite direction of where the team would be headed about twenty minutes before they left. Large herds moved toward the flashing, beeping tennis balls, but these were much larger herds than they had seen in the area before. Also, the sound didn't carry as far through the dense crowds, and the wind and noise of the thunderstorms further diminished the reach of the beeping sounds. Ever since the makeshift bridge across the river had been destroyed, the masses of zombies that had stretched for miles down the West Side Highway had slowly begun to disperse, and far too many of them had filtered into the neighborhood around Columbia.

"There's going to be hell to pay getting through these bastards," the Ranger said, lowering his binoculars after surveying as much of their route as he could see from the window which faced north.

Martha then meekly raised her hand as if she was in elementary school trying to ask permission to go to the bathroom.

"You have something you want to ask?" Pete said in a kind tone, but it sounded a lot like a parent talking to a child, even though Martha was twice his age.

"Well, I, uh, was just wondering if the SZP wouldn't help protect us?" she said in her librarian-like voice.

"The what?" Pete asked, not sure if he heard her correctly.

"The *Synthetic ZIPs Pheromone* that Dr. Devereaux had me synthesize a few weeks ago," Martha replied, as if everyone was supposed to know what she was talking about.

Pete, Max, and the other Columbia people all glanced at one another and shrugged their shoulders or shook their heads to indicate they didn't have a clue what SZP was, or what it was supposed to do.

"Uh, Martha, would you be so kind as to explain to us all what SZP is?" Max said nicely, but with a knitted brow and rapidly darkening features.

Was there something that could have protected them—and saved Erin's life—on their way back from sending Pete on his way? Martha could sense the tension in the room and it slowly dawned on her that Devereaux hadn't told anyone about the pheromone project.

"Don't blame *me!*" she suddenly shouted, taking everyone aback, as her pale cheeks flushed a mottled red and tears welled up in her eyes. "I just did my work. I just did what Dr. Devereaux told me to do!"

"I see what you mean," Cam whispered to Pete in the midst of Martha's outburst.

Becks took a chance and stepped forward and put her arm around the flustered woman's shoulders and offered her a water bottle.

"No one's blaming *you* for anything," Becks began in the practiced soothing manner she had perfected after years of working in the emergency room of Nyack Hospital, where she had to deal with all kinds of freaked out people. "Why don't you just have a seat and start from the beginning?"

Martha took a few sips of water and perched her flabby rear end on the edge of a lab chair. Her voice was loud at first, but quickly settled into her soft librarian register as she explained the SZP project. Though a little scatterbrained, Martha was very knowledgeable and had a sharp mind— much sharper than anyone realized.

Dr. Devereaux had come to her with an idea several weeks earlier. They had all isolated the ZIPs' pheromone months ago, but under the circumstances, couldn't possibly extract enough of it from the zombies to create an effective masking agent—to be able to "smell like a zombie" and thereby be able to avoid being attacked.

However, in one of Devereaux's flashes of brilliance, he conceived of a way of synthesizing the critical chemical compounds of the ZIPs' pheromone. It wouldn't be an exact match, but hopefully it would be close enough to make an effective biochemical camouflage. Unfortunately, with limited resources, and after several failed attempts, Martha had only been able to produce a few drops of pure synthetic pheromone, and it hadn't been tested yet with any zombies, but she was certain it would work.

"Certain enough for us to trust our lives with it?" the Ranger asked, suspicious of anything that couldn't be cocked and fired.

"Dr. Devereaux was *never* wrong about such things!" Martha declared indignantly, displaying yet another side of her multiple personalities that was just a slightly more controlled version of her previous outburst.

Pete then initiated a brief brainstorming session to see how best to utilize the limited SZP they had. After a slew of complex suggestions such as creating aerosols with laser-targeting, inert propellant dispensers, Cam interrupted and asked why they simply couldn't put a drop on some gauze or cotton wrapped around the end of a yardstick?

"Yeah, that could work, too," Pete said with a bemused expression, realizing that they were sometimes all a little too smart for their own good.

Martha would be in charge of the "pheromone wand," and keep a plastic baggie over the treated gauze to protect it from the rain until it needed to be used. However, as she had never "been out in the field" before, there was considerable concern about her ability to handle this important assignment, but, as everyone else would be needed to fight, the task of wielding the wand fell to the emotionally unstable lab assistant. Everyone quietly prayed it would not prove to be a fatal mistake.

The Ranger and Mad Max were first out of the door, and caught a faceful of wind-driven rain. Cam and Becks followed on either side of Martha, with Pete and Julian bringing up the rear. While the others were less than thrilled with the pelting drops of water, Becks found them to be oddly reassuring and helped her to focus. Her nerves were still far more fragile than she would ever admit, and the discomfort of the rain was a valuable distraction.

Their route was initially relatively clear as they made their way to Fort Washington Avenue where they would start heading north, but there were plenty of mobile corpses ahead of them. Fortunately, as zombies possessed a general aversion to water, many kept themselves pressed against buildings and huddled in doorways to avoid the pouring rain. Also, for those who had switched more than a year ago, the blinding flashes of lightning played upon their sensitivity to bright light, and those zombies also sought some shelter or put their hands and arms in front of their faces.

Anything that helped lower the number of zombies was welcomed, but of course, not even the nastiest thunderstorm could counteract the force of hunger. As soon as fresh meat passed by, these dripping wet, partially decayed figures staggered out of doorways and from under awnings to join in the pursuit of their potential meal.

Max used Mama to deadly effect, but while his right hand swung the battle axe, he needed his left hand to hold over his mouth to stifle his maniacal laughter. He simply couldn't control himself every time Mama sunk deep into a cranium—especially whenever bits of brain spilled out or an eye was cleaved from its socket.

The Ranger's weapon of choice was naturally the M9 bayonet attached to the end of his M4 rifle. While lacking the skull-splintering power of Mama, the bayonet thrust of the muscular Ranger had an equally devastating effect on flesh and bone. Sticky Pete used his homemade spear, Cam had a machete, and Becks had her favorite commando knife. Regardless of the personal choice of weapons, everyone was trying to move quickly and kill as quietly as possible to avoid drawing even bigger crowds.

It was tempting to do an all-out sprint, but as they would be traveling over a mile, there was no way Julian and Martha would be able to keep up the pace over that distance. As it was, the two were already moving too slowly, prompting the Ranger to bark at them to hurry up and move their lazy asses, which was probably not the best strategy. Martha got flustered and dropped the wand, but fortunately it remained dry. Julian probably wet himself, but in the downpour, no one could tell for sure.

For the length of two entire blocks, the group crawled along the street side of the continuous line of parked cars, as masses of zombies huddled in packs on the sidewalks under tattered construction and business awnings or the brick archways of apartment building entrances. To everyone's credit, the broken glass and debris that cut their hands and knees was borne in stoic silence.

Just past the intersection with 171st Street, about 50 zombies were trying to jam into a clear glass bus stop shelter designed for no more than a dozen people, and there was no way to pass them without being seen. In the middle of the intersection, there were several cars at odd angles in the street, creating something of a zigzagging bottleneck through which they would have to pass single-file, right into the crowd of zombies. The sidewalks were not a better option, as hundreds more still clung to the fronts of buildings on both sides of the street. As the group whispered ideas for their plan of attack—basically having five fighters rushing headlong into the mini-herd ten times their number—Becks had a better idea.

"Thermopylae," Becks said, to blank or puzzled expressions, and then continued. "You know, the Spartans, the Persians, the narrow pass?"

"You mean like that movie *300*?" Max asked. "Yeah, I saw that on Netflix. Remember that movie, Pete?"

"Oh, that movie was awesome. You sure we didn't rent that on DVD?" Pete responded, going completely off track.

"Yes, yes, awesome movie," Becks snapped, losing patience. "The point is, rather than us running into that crowd one at a time, why don't we draw the crowd through that gap in the cars and bring them to us single file?"

"Sounds like a plan, let's go," the Ranger said, jumping to his feet and sprinting toward the cars in the intersection.

"Wait, what?" Cam said, surprised by the Ranger's rash action. "Shit, I guess it's go time."

The rest of the group hurried to join the Ranger and take up defensive positions crouched behind the cars. The key was to attract the attention of the zombies at the bus stop, without riling up all the others in the surrounding area. The Ranger accomplished that by throwing a broken bottle at a tall, male zombie in a suit, while softly saying, "Hey, asshole."

The tall zombie immediately headed their way, and after bouncing off a couple of fenders and bumpers, found the gap between the cars and stumbled through, right into the waiting bayonet of the Ranger. A stout female followed, only to fall to a devastating lateral blow from Mama that sent the top two inches of her skull and brains flying onto the windshield of a silver Toyota Prius. Cam and Becks easily handled the next pair, and then Pete joined in with his spear, as he secretly pretended to be the Spartan King Leonidas, *with* the six-pack abs, of course.

"Clear these bodies to the side," Becks ordered Julian and Martha, who seemed more than content to let everyone else do the dirty work.

As the two timid members of the team dragged the grisly, bloody corpses out of the way to make room for more grisly, bloody corpses, the rest of the team took turns thinning the mini-herd. But after about twenty-five kills, the other natives on the street were getting restless and were starting to shamble off the sidewalks wherever they could squeeze through the lines of cars.

"We're running out of time!" Martha shouted, as she started to lose it.

"Shut up and hold your position!" the Ranger yelled, but to no avail.

Martha grabbed the yardstick with the pheromone gauze, yanked off the baggie, and headed through the gap toward the remaining crowd. A male zombie chef in a very soiled apron and hat had started to enter the gap, but when Martha thrust the gauze under his nose, he stopped, tilted his head and rolled his eyes as if he was tasting an exquisite French sauce, and actually took a few steps backward! Waving the yardstick in front of half a dozen more zombies, they passively turned and went back under the bus shelter.

"Come on, move your lazy asses!" Martha screamed to the group, urging them forward with her free hand.

"Well I'll be damned!" the Ranger said in astonishment, as he was next through the gap, quickly followed by all the others.

Martha swung the stick back and forth a few more times, just to make sure none of the zombies would follow, then replaced the plastic bag and rejoined the group. Everyone made sure to tell her she had done a great job, but she insisted *all* of the credit should go to Dr. Devereaux.

The celebration ended quickly, however, as the wall of zombies ahead of them was much larger than anyone had ever encountered.

Chapter 13

Word of the massive herd coming up the Palisades Interstate Parkway spread rapidly through the communities of Tappan, Orangeburg, Sparkill, Piermont, and Palisades. Though the population was sparse, the residents were determined not to lose what they had fought so hard to regain once they began turning the tide of the apocalypse.

Barricades of boulders, cars, furniture, logs, and fencing were piled up at all the entrance and exit ramps in southern Rockland County, in a "not in my backyard" mentality. Of course, that just meant that the herd would go farther north to the towns of Pearl River, Nanuet, and New City, so the people there also began barricading ramps and roads where zombies might wander off into *their* backyards.

The Army and the local militias promptly knocked down all the hastily-constructed barricades, as they might need those access points to battle the herd with whatever strategy was finally decided upon. Everything was in an extreme state of confusion and panic, and no one was quite sure if it was even possible to combat the hundreds of thousands of zombies.

Becks and her group stopped in their tracks as they wondered if this was as far as they could go. There was a small park on the northwest corner of the intersection, and for some reason it looked as if every zombie in the neighborhood was trying to get in. Perhaps some morsel of fresh meat was discovered in the park, which had sent the herd surging toward it.

A low stone wall surrounded the park, and it was almost comical as the herd inexorably pushed forward and the front line of staggering corpses was flipped headfirst over the wall. Barely had that line struggled to their feet, when the next group of zombie acrobats came tumbling over the wall.

However, at the sight of living, breathing, delicious humans, the tide turned. As the herd in the street lurched toward them, the crowd in the park started pushing to get out, and the line that had most recently gotten to their feet after falling over the wall, was now pushed back over it onto the sidewalk, to repeat the entire ridiculous process in reverse. But no one had the time or inclination to laugh—it would be suicide to take on this mass of undead humanity.

"Right, right, right!" Sticky Pete shouted, as he motioned everyone to go east on 173rd Street.

The first few hundred feet of this block were clear, as the smooth walls of the buildings on both sides were uninterrupted by doorways or recesses of any kind, not offering any shelter for the zombies. Up ahead were some gated alleys, but they moved quietly and quickly enough to not attract the attention of the shadowy figures lurking in their depths. Then on their left, was a schoolyard—a schoolyard filled with dozens of ragged little undead children.

The entire team paused as one to stare in horror as these ravenous mini-zombies pressed their cheeks and hands against the chain link fence—the fence which once protected them in their joyful recess playtime, but now held them back from mercilessly falling upon the adults. Many of the children pressed so hard that decaying pieces of lips, noses, and fingertips were rubbed clean off and fell to the pavement in ghastly, little piles. A bright bolt of lightning and a rumbling clap of thunder jolted the group out of its state of shock, and they hurried on their way, although each one knew these were images they would never be able to entirely erase from their memories.

Then, unfortunately, the relatively sparsely populated side street opened up onto the wide intersection of Broadway, and even wider herds stretching to the south and east as far as the eye could see. They would be going north, which didn't have as many zombies, but before anyone could get too complacent, the Ranger reminded everyone, "Never leave a sizable force of the enemy in your rear."

Max snickered at the unintended, lewd, double entendre, but Pete shot him a sharp look and he clammed up.

"We need a diversion or distraction to keep them from following us," the Ranger continued. "If we run into any delays or impediments ahead, we will be trapped. Mission over."

"How about taking a page from the Becks' School of Pyrotechnics?" Cam asked, pointing to a gas station just up ahead on the right, and referring to her scorched earth policy while trying to survive in the New Jersey suburbs.

"There's no power," Julian said, as panic raised his voice at least an octave. "You won't be able to pump out any gas."

"No need," Cam responded, taking Julian by the arm and pulling him forward, afraid the young doctor was about to bolt. "We will use the storage tanks in the ground, but we will need something dry to start a fire. Look for clothing or papers, anything combustible."

As the team members all rushed for the gas station, they briefly stopped here and there to pick up scraps of cardboard and newspaper from under cars, and jammed them in their jackets to keep them dry. Martha found a weathered corpse in a doorway and tore off its clothes like a crazed sex maniac.

Once under the awning of the gas station, Cam directed Pete and Max to handle stragglers, while Becks and the others tied all the refuse together in bundles with the clothing, and he and the Ranger tried to pry up the heavy, metal lid that covered the massive underground storage tank. Using a piece of pipe to finally pop the lid, the strong cloud of escaping petroleum fumes was encouraging. The Ranger tossed a glass bottle into the tank and the gratifying splashing sound indicated there was a still plenty of gasoline to create an effective diversion.

"Hurry up, god damn it!" Max shouted, as he swung Mama back and forth amongst the skulls of the encroaching herd. "We can't keep this up much longer."

Once the bundles of paper and cloth were assembled, Becks grabbed a bottle of 10W-30 oil from a rack and stabbed it with her commando knife. Then she drizzled the oil over the bundles to make sure they would burn well. She was fully prepared to stay behind and drop the flaming bundles in the storage tank, but Cam literally smacked the idea out of her with the swat to her butt.

"You never could outrun me, Trues. Hell, no high school kid in the Hudson Valley, could," he said with that maddening—and thoroughly charming—gloating tone and expression. "You all start clearing a path north and I'll be right behind you."

Cam wanted the herd to get as close as possible, so if there was any kind of explosion along with the fire, it would maximize casualties. Becks whispered, "Don't be stupid," and then she and the rest of the team started jogging northward. Groups of half a dozen or more zombies were everywhere, and they fought when they had to, and just ran where they could. But with every step, Becks glanced over her shoulder to see if Cam was coming.

Tense seconds ticked by and she was about to turn back, when finally, she saw Cam running like the track star he had been. But he was also yelling something and wildly waving his arms toward the ground.

"Get down, take cover!" he shouted frantically, as the team members all threw themselves behind cars and trucks.

Before Cam could shout his warning again, a thunderous sound—that Becks could only imagine was what an erupting volcano sounded like—shredded the air, a split second before a brilliant flash of crimson seemed to ignite the very atmosphere around them.

The devastating explosion propelled Cam fifteen feet through the air, landing him face first in the blood and guts of a freshly-killed female zombie in lingerie and stiletto-heeled leather boots. But that was nothing compared to the gas station pumps, pavement, and office that launched straight up as if trying to achieve orbit. The blast eviscerated hundreds, if not thousands of the tightly-packed zombies, and leveled two, five-story brick buildings, a small white church, and several other buildings on the east side of the street behind the gas station.

Across Broadway on the west side, the explosion compromised the structural integrity of a 12-story brick building enough that it began to creak and groan and sway. Then, almost as if in slow motion, the startled team watched in amazement as it tipped over as a single unit, then shattered in a deafening shower of bricks as it slammed to the ground.

If the gas station explosion, subsequent hellfire, and towering plume of smoke wasn't enough of a distraction and deterrent to the thousands of zombies left in the herd, the impediment of a prone 12-story building damming the width of Broadway would keep anything from pursuing the team.

When Becks and the Ranger ran back to help Cam to his feet, he just smiled awkwardly and said, "I guess there was more gasoline than I thought."

"That's the understatement of the year!" Becks said, wanting to give him a hug, but deciding he was covered with way too much of a sticky, gooey zombie mess.

The Armageddon-scale diversion—which blew out windows for several blocks—drew herds from all directions, including those in their path ahead. It was decided that rather than "swim upstream" through the approaching zombies, they instead would hunker down somewhere and wait until the herd passed.

Trying several buildings on the block, they had to backtrack a bit before they found the doors to a magnificent old movie theater–turned-church were unlocked, and the team resumed their original formation to enter. The lobby was like an ornate palace, harking back to the golden age of motion pictures in the 1930s, when desperate people sought refuge from the brutal realities of the Great Depression. Now, these seven people sought refuge from the Great Apocalypse, and the splendor of their surroundings was in stark contrast to the blood and filth that covered them all.

Someone, perhaps from the former congregation of the church, had crudely painted several signs on cardboard and propped them up on folding chairs by the entrance.

"Yea, though I walk through the valley of the shadow of death, I will fear no evil," one sign read.

"Blessed is the man who remains steadfast under trial," another proclaimed in dripping, blue paint.

The third, and largest, sat in the middle and exclaimed, "God bless our immortal souls—now go kick some zombie ass!"

"Amen to *that*!" the Ranger whispered, as they slowly circled the lobby to make sure it was secure. After they were certain nothing living or dead would sneak up on them, they dropped their gear and found some musty, but comfortable, chairs and couches on which to rest. Even though they hadn't traveled very far, they had done a lot of killing in that short distance and it had already taken a toll.

Becks' knife-wielding arm was sore, and she was soaked in both rain and sweat. Her long hours in the lab had clearly left her out of fighting shape. Martha looked dazed and wild-eyed. Julian grabbed his knees and pulled them tight against his chest, and rocked slowly back and forth, trembling. Sticky Pete and Max sat in stoic silence, as dangerous supply runs for them had been a weekly occurrence. Cam and the Ranger actually looked as though they were enjoying themselves.

After about ten minutes, Max cautiously approached the front doors, not wanting to draw any attention. He looked up and down Broadway to determine how many zombies had passed, and how many more were going to pass by their location. When he returned to the group to give his report, a sharp explosion ripped through the air, instinctively sending everyone to the floor. A few seconds later there was a second explosion, and third, and then a fourth, even louder than the first three.

"Cars?" Becks asked, as they all looked at each other with puzzled expressions.

A discussion ensued in which they decided that the spreading conflagration was consuming cars, and that any that had enough gas in their tanks were exploding. However, it was also possible that some of the destroyed buildings had sufficient natural gas left in their pipes to set off the last, and loudest, explosion.

"I guess this is the diversion that keeps on giving!" Cam said proudly.

A second later they all flinched as several more exploding automobiles splintered apart and sent shrapnel into the gathering crowds of zombies.

It was an unusual phenomenon Becks had observed in New Jersey, when she set fire to cars and houses. The herds were attracted by the light and sounds, but when crowds pushed forward, those in front were helplessly shoved directly into the flames and immolated. But the fires she had set were nothing compared to the block-long blaze that threatened to spread unchecked, even in this driving rainstorm.

"You always have to try to outdo me, don't you?" Becks said smiling, as she tossed an empty water bottle at his grinning face.

Max finally explained that within five or ten minutes, he estimated that the largest concentrations of zombies in the area would be to their south, pressing tightly against the collapsed brick building across the road, which itself was now ablaze.

"The more of the stupid bastards who set themselves on fire, the better!" Max exclaimed, rubbing his Mama-swinging shoulder, which had seen more action today than in the last several months combined.

The Ranger instructed everyone to have one of the granola bars they all carried, and to drink a bottle of water. Then he requested that Pete and Max refresh their memories about the terrain ahead and what to expect. He also strongly cautioned everyone to stick closely together, as the boat would not wait for stragglers.

"OK," he said, after the brief meeting, in the tone of a man who expected to be obeyed, "Gear up and let's all get to the river in one piece."

The heat from the conflagration was palpable, even at this distance, as they stepped out onto the sidewalk. In fact, it was generating a steamy wind blowing north. The rain didn't feel so cold anymore; it felt refreshing in that oppressive heat.

The mass of zombies was now to their south and continued to move toward the flames, oblivious to the fact that they were about to be incinerated. That all-too-familiar stench of burning flesh was now competing with the smoking petroleum flames for most offensive odor. But the team was moving north, as fast as it could go, away from it all.

Becks quickly lost track of the streets as they were constantly weaving east and west to avoid solid jams of cars and even more solid herds of zombies. For every block north, it seemed they had to go two or three blocks out of their way. Everyone was getting exhausted from the distance and constant hard fighting. The only good part was that Becks was too tired and too busy to have time to think about the situation—she was just reacting, which is exactly what she hoped would happen.

"Fuck this!" Max finally said, barely able to raise Mama above his head anymore. "I'm getting us some wheels."

Max ran ahead to a city bus that was diagonally across both lanes of the street, and had its front end rammed into the side of a minivan. He paid no attention to the six or seven occupants stuck inside the minivan, weakly, but desperately, pounding their decaying fists against the windows trying to have their first meal since they all died and switched.

The driver of the bus could not be so easily ignored, however, if Max wanted to commandeer the vehicle. He was more vigorous than the minivan occupants, as he had obviously had a substantial supply of extra fat before going zombie, as the hanging folds of now empty skin attested. The ZIPs had been feeding off that fat, waiting for the day for someone to release the bus driver from his seat belt. Max was happy to oblige, but only after cleaving the man's skull almost in two.

Tossing the body out the door to the pavement, Max then reached for the keys and crossed his fingers. Unfortunately, the battery was dead, but one of the Columbia students had designed a device that when inserted into the socket of an auxiliary power port actually jumpstarted the vehicle. Coaxing the transmission into first, Max pushed the minivan ahead until it fell over sideways and clear of his path. Next popping it into reverse, he burned rubber backing up to the rest of his team members. They all gladly piled into the bus and out of the rain, and away from the never-ending zombie packs.

"Why didn't we do this sooner?" Martha angrily mumbled under her breath as she plopped down into a seat, wiping the profuse sweat from her face.

Max bit his tongue and didn't dignify her remark with a response, as everyone knew damn well most of the streets were too clogged with abandoned cars to have any hope of getting very far. Still, even to catch a short break and drive a few blocks was a very welcome respite. Even Cam and the Ranger needed to catch their breaths.

Progress was slow, as the massive city bus acted more like a plow shoving cars out of the way, but progress was steady nonetheless. Once or twice they had to take a side street detour, as even the mighty bus didn't have the strength to push half a block of cars.

It more than had enough strength, however, to mow down large numbers of zombies. In fact, Max went out of his way—and goosed the gas pedal in the process—to flatten somewhere in the neighborhood of 200 of the "ugly bastards" as he called one group he ran down, and then backed over, twice, just for good measure.

They actually got a lot farther than they expected, but somewhere on Cabrini Boulevard near 190th Street their luck finally ran out. The narrow street was packed with cars and completely impassable. Trying to back out of the street also proved futile as several flat tires from all the debris made maneuvering next to impossible, and Max somehow managed to wedge the bus between a brick wall and a sanitation truck.

"Sorry folks, last stop," Max shouted. "Everybody out."

Fortunately, the zombie population appeared to be sparse here, but unfortunately, it was time to leave the streets and head west for the river. That meant that they would have to hop a wrought iron fence and go down a steep, wooded hill to the Henry Hudson Parkway below, which was thick with zombies in both the northbound and southbound sides. The Ranger got a call that the boat from West Point was about ten minutes out and he gave them the team's current position, and where by the river they hoped to end up.

Pete suggested that the boat should first go further to the south, and make a lot of noise to draw off some of the vast horde. If that diversion could make even a small break in the line of ravenous killers, it could be a lifesaver.

The river was just on the other side of the highway, and the highway was just at the bottom of the hill, which, thanks to all the rain had become a treacherous downhill slalom of mud. Martha promptly went down and slid face first into a tree. As Becks and Cam tried to help the dazed and bloodied woman to her feet, they both lost their footing. Becks slid fifteen feet into a fallen tree and had the wind knocked out of her. Cam managed to grab onto a sapling to stop his fall, but then the whole damn tree pulled right out of the soil. He careened backwards into a big oak and saw stars for a full minute after the impact.

Julian was alternately screaming and cursing as he fell repeatedly. The Ranger couldn't stay on his feet, either, and made a rude acquaintance with a couple of maple trees. Even Max, with the lowest center of gravity, tumbled several times, actually going completely head over heels into an old stump.

"Everyone on your asses," Pete shouted, realizing that trying to walk down the slippery slope was going to get someone seriously injured.

Even with everyone trying to slide on their butts down the hill, it was dangerous business, and by the time they made it to level ground, all of them were winded, and not one of them wasn't bloody and bruised. They weren't in any shape to continue without a breather, so they huddled together behind a clump of trees, and out of sight of the mass of zombies on the Henry Hudson Parkway just a short distance in front of them. They sat in silence, except for their heavy breathing, and let the pouring rain wash the dirt from their wounds. Minutes ticked by, and finally that wonderful sound of the boat from West Point was heard roaring along the river. And what a boat!

It had actually been a Coast Guard vessel—Defender class—but since no one had been left in the Coast Guard, the Army had appropriated a few of them from New York Harbor right before they blew the bridge. The Defender was capable of ripping through the water at over 50 miles-per-hour, and its .50 cal machine gun made its own statement for anyone wishing to challenge its authority. It would still take three hours to get to Albany, but what a way to travel! If they could all reach the boat, that is.

The Defender skimmed across the water toward the proposed pickup point, and then veered right to hug the shore and make some noise, which it did quite effectively with an air horn. Immediately, zombies who had been milling about on the highway all turned *en masse* and headed south toward the blaring sound. The team would probably have to wait hours for the Henry Hudson Parkway to clear—hours they couldn't waste—so they just would have to pick a thin spot or gap they hoped would open up with the uneven pace of the various zombies who were in all manner of decomposition.

Some looked to have switched on day one of the infection, and had bits and pieces falling off of them as they staggered laboriously along. The majority was a bit "younger" and traveled better, although their general lack of food seemed to make them slower than the "country zombies." Of course, no one wanted a fast zombie, but the team was hoping they would all move along a little more quickly.

After waiting impatiently for about fifteen minutes, an opening began to appear in the northbound lane, which was closest to Becks' group. The southbound side was still relatively congested, but the numbers had definitely diminished.

"I think it's now or never," Becks concluded, once again sliding her commando knife out of its sheath.

As they were all bloody and caked with mud, Julian suggested that they stagger slowly through the crowd and pretend to be zombies. Unfortunately, there was the problem of smelling like humans—or more accurately—not smelling like a zombie. The ZIPs pheromone on the gauze had become too diluted in the rain to be effective anymore, so they really had only one option to cross the highway—run as fast, and fight as hard, as they could.

The Ranger quickly delineated the plan—run and fight across the northbound lanes of the highway, and then regroup in the wooded area in between the north and south lanes. There they would wait for another thin spot in the herd, and cross the southbound lanes. Regroup again in the woods between the southbound lanes and the railroad tracks, before the final push across the tracks, through the last line of trees, and head to the river. It sounded good; now they would just have to do it all while staying alive in the process.

It didn't seem possible, but the rain and wind suddenly increased in intensity. Water running into their eyes made it difficult to see, but if the humans were having trouble, it had to be much worse for the zombies, who were already visually challenged. Becks started to recall a fascinating study conducted by an ophthalmologist at West Point two months earlier that illustrated how ZIPs compromised human eyesight—indeed, all of our human senses. This mental journey was something Becks often did in times of great stress, as picturing charts, diagrams, and statistics helped her cope.

So as her mind's eye traced the slope of the red line on the chart which indicated the decrease of visual acuity vs. time in those test subjects who had switched between six to twelve months earlier, she drove her commando knife deep into the eye socket of a woman wearing a blouse made of a bright bird-patterned fabric.

When she recounted the two columns of numbers detailing the raw data of the test results—and was that a standard deviation of 3.7 or 3.6, she wondered?—she was plunging her knife through the external acoustic meatus—the ear hole—of a large man in stained, yellow cycling shorts and a jersey, whom she had knocked to the pavement with a brutal, ligament-shattering kick to the junction between the femur and tibia—the side of the knee.

Other facts and figures came to mind as she became a killing machine; rescuing Julian, not once, but three times, which in such a short span of distance was something of an achievement, being capable of getting himself into peril that many times.

Cam dragged Martha along as he registered his own large number of kills, but his mind was always focused on the intimate details of how his machete sliced through muscles, tendons, and bones—how each sounded while being cut, and the deep, pungent smells of the blood and other fluids that subsequently gushed out. Everyone had their own way of dealing with killing.

Fortunately, zombies usually favored pavement to the woods, but as the team regrouped and caught their breath 30 feet off the road, there were still a dozen or so stragglers, driven to try to get some shelter from the rain under the trees, that needed to be dispatched. Even the bayonet thrust of the Ranger was now labored, however, and exhaustion threatened to end their mission within sight of their objective.

"I'm going to have to start shooting," Max confessed, huffing and puffing, his face flushed and dripping in sweat and blood, "I just can't swing my Mama anymore! Not one more skull!"

Everyone agreed, it had to be pistols from here to the river, as aching muscles and extreme fatigue had left them all feeling like they had just gone 15 rounds with a heavyweight champ.

"I don't know if I have enough ammo, or enough strength to even use my guns," Pete moaned, already running on fumes from his paddling marathon and lack of sleep.

"We can't stop now, we just can't," the Ranger said, but with less of his former commanding voice, and more as if he was trying to convince himself.

"Maybe I can help with this," Cam said, looking unusually sheepish.

"What can you do?" Becks asked suspiciously.

Reaching into one of his pockets, he pulled out a zip lock bag which had a bunch of little twisted bundles of something wrapped in what looked like that red, flimsy firecracker paper.

"What are you going to do, try to scare them off with homemade firecrackers?" the Ranger snapped derisively.

"Well, these are homemade firecrackers all right," Cam said with a devilish grin, regaining a little swagger, "but they are for us. The Monk— a friend of mine—whipped these little babies up to give a quick boost in times of extreme danger. I don't know what's in them—and I probably don't want to know—but you snort one of these and you could run head first through a cinderblock wall."

"If they get me through that wall of zombies, that's good enough for me," Martha declared, as she pulled one of The Monk's firecrackers out of the bag and snorted it like a pro, much to everyone's astonishment. "Oh! OH MY!"

Martha's eyes opened unnaturally wide, and she started rubbing her hands together so quickly it looked like she was trying to start a fire with them.

"What the hell are you all waiting for!?" Martha shouted, looking every inch as though she was capable, and eager, to run through a wall.

The Ranger and Max each quickly grabbed one of the red paper twists, and carefully unwrapped them while trying to shield the contents from the rain. A few deep, short snorts and they were also bug-eyed and raring to go.

Becks hesitated, but not because she didn't need the boost—it was because she had never snorted any sort of substance in her life, and she was embarrassed to admit it. Fortunately, Pete was first to confess the same thing, with Julian following. So there, in the midst of a violent thunderstorm, surrounded by ravenous zombies, in the ruins of what was once the greatest city in the world, Cam had to give a brief demo on Drug Snorting 101.

Becks wasn't quite sure if it had been powdered lava or TNT she had just introduced into her nasal passages, but the top of her head suddenly felt like the lid of a pressure cooker, and she needed a way to let off steam. She also wasn't exactly sure who shouted "Geronimo!"—it could have even been her, and it could have been all of them—as their team burst out of the woods, slashing and hacking and stabbing everything in sight.

In the ensuing melee, Max slipped and fell on a slick pile of intestines he had just caused to spill out from a young man wearing a t-shirt with a peace symbol—a symbol which was now two semi-circles with a bloody, gaping hole in the middle. In his highly-altered state, Max found this all hilariously funny and didn't seem particularly concerned that an unusually tall, well-built zombie with a very prominent jaw had knelt down and was about to sink his very large teeth into Max's very exposed neck.

Just as the tips of the teeth met his skin, a distant shot rang out. A hole suddenly appeared in the zombie's left temple. Dark blood and greenish ZIPs fluid gushed out into Max's face. Choking on all the nasty bodily fluids that had poured into his open mouth, Max sat bolt upright, gagging and spitting out the foul substances. Then he looked around to see who had fired the shot, but the rest of the team was just entering the woods, and no one had their guns drawn.

"I'm telling you, someone shot him!" Max exclaimed in his 20-cups-of-coffee hyper-agitated state.

"You're crazy!" the Ranger shouted much too loudly. "We're all crazy from these damned firecrackers. None of us took a shot, and the boat is too far south."

"I'm telling you, *someone took a shot!*" Max insisted, but was way too amped up to stand around and argue about it.

Ignoring Max as best he could, the Ranger got on the radio to let the boat know that they were almost in position by the river. Only the railroad tracks, a thin line of trees, and a footpath remained before the final ten yards of trees and rocks on the bank of the river, and from what they could see, their path looked relatively clear. However, the boat informed him that heaps of debris from the collapse of the George Washington foot bridge had spread out like a tsunami in all directions and the entire length of the riverbank on the Manhattan side was littered with tree limbs, screen doors, Badminton rackets, plastic shopping carts, torn clothing, and futons, all caked in a putrid-smelling mud, mixed with chunks of burned and decayed flesh. It would be tricky footing, and completely disgusting, but it would be the last few yards before they were free of this hellish island.

The train tracks had just a few stragglers, and no one needed to draw blood. The footpath was similarly no problem. As the team entered the last strip of woods going down to the water, they all began to breathe easier and relax—or as close to relaxed as they could get while still jacked up on The Monk's firecrackers.

The roar of the Defender drawing closer was also a comforting sound, and Becks was finally allowing herself to make that little mental check mark that this part of the mission, at least, was a success. This had been much more of a strain than she would allow herself to admit—her first time "back out there" since her ordeal in New Jersey, and more zombie kills than she could count. As relieved as she was, however, she had no plans of patting herself on the back until the entire mission was complete, and that included the eradication of the hundreds of thousands of zombies who had escaped Manhattan.

The rain even seemed to be letting up a bit as the bedraggled team members emerged from the tree line. There was a tangled mass at the water's edge, like a garbage dump had exploded—which in essence, was exactly what happened. Waving enthusiastically to the crew members on the Defender, which was now just about 50 yards off, Cam took the first tenuous steps onto the debris. The first couple of yards required a delicate balancing act, but then he seemed to find firm footing on a mattress stained brown, green, and red.

"I don't even want to know where this thing has been," Cam said laughing, as he bounced up and down like a little kid—an amphetamine-infused little kid, "but it looks like we have a gangplank to freedom."

Becks was about to tell him to be careful and stop acting like a dumb ass, but instead she started screaming.

"Look out! Behind you, Cam!" Becks yelled, as a rotting hand was reaching up over the edge of the filthy mattress.

Before anyone could react, the hand grasped Cam's right ankle and yanked him backwards into the water. Becks, the Ranger, Max, and Pete sprang forward to try to rescue him, slipping and falling on the treacherous tangle of debris, which suddenly began writhing and shifting as if it was alive.

"Zombies!" Julian started screaming in his high-pitched hysteria. "The debris is filled with zombies!"

Thousands and thousands of zombies had been on the makeshift foot path when the helicopter blew it to bits, and their bodies had been enmeshed with all of the garbage as it rushed out to sea, and also blown backwards to the riverbanks. Arms and legs and heads now rose up out of the muck between couch cushions, branches, and umbrellas. It seemed as if a hundred hands were now grabbing at everyone as they desperately tried to scramble across the pile and get to Cam, who still hadn't come to the surface. Becks was frantic and slashed her way through the many body parts trying to pull her down, and jabbed relentlessly into the gnashing jaws attempting to eat her. If she was getting bitten, she didn't feel it, as panic had completely overwhelmed her senses.

Cam's head briefly rose above the surface as his bloodied face contorted and gasped for air. The Ranger, with his long reach, almost got a hold of his shoulder, but at the last second he was yanked back down below the murky water. Everyone was yelling, the debris pile was starting to break up in the skirmish, and Max and Pete were now shoulder-deep in garbage, struggling to get free and keep their heads above water. They were both screaming in pain as they were being bitten by the many mouths hidden in the debris, as well as being cut and stabbed by the sharp edges of all that junk.

The commander of the Defender, a petite, yet rock-hard-bodied Hispanic woman named Tejada, kept her cool and ordered her crew to take a shot only if there was a clear shot to be had—which under the circumstances, was almost impossible. Not knowing what kind of dangerous debris was under the water, she couldn't risk bringing the boat in too close. However, she was not going to just sit there and watch the entire team die right in front of her, so she ordered the grappling hook launcher to be aimed toward the line of debris just to the south of the team.

Julian and Martha finally joined in the melee, and thanks to the continued benefits of pharmaceutical courage, they managed to pull Pete free of the debris, but it looked like he was bleeding in a dozen different places. Max was stuck fast, and he was howling as a set of teeth had clamped onto his thigh. Martha recklessly drew her pistol and aimed it somewhere in the vicinity of Max's thigh/crotch and prepared to fire.

"Whoa, whoa, WHOA!" Max shrieked, grabbing Martha's wildly trembling hand and shoving the barrel of the gun onto the head of whatever male or female zombie was dining on his leg.

With the skull of his attacker shattered, Max had a little more wiggle room, but he still couldn't pull himself free, and continued to struggle to keep from being pulled below the water level.

Becks and the Ranger both dove into the water to help Cam, but there was zero visibility. Flailing around searching for him, she found a man struggling a few feet down. Feeling along his torso, she found his head and thrust her arm securely around his neck. Becks' lungs were burning for oxygen as she planted her feet against a rock or tree trunk and used her legs to propel the two of them to the surface.

Her relief at breaking above the water and gulping in a deep breath was short lived, however, as she realized she was holding onto the slimy, rotting zombie who had pulled Cam into the water. He was way too big for her to handle—and too slippery—and he quickly was able to flip her over and push her back under the water, all the while as his jaws snapped at her. She fought with all her strength to hold him back, but he was standing on debris with his head out of the water, while her face was a foot below, and lack of breath was quickly weakening her.

Just as things started to go black, a spurt of a lumpy red substance hit the water just above Becks' eyes, and the zombie's grip went limp. Bursting to the surface, Becks gasped for air, as her attacker, who was now oozing blood and brains from a sizable hole and his forehead, fell with a mighty splash.

"Nice shot," Tejada shouted to her crew, and was then puzzled when they responded that no one had fired.

A hand grabbed Becks by the collar from behind and she started fighting until she heard Julian yelling that it was just him.

"Cam, where's Cam?" Becks shouted in between gagging and coughing, as she was rapidly losing hope

"He's okay! The Ranger has him," Julian yelled back over all the noise and chaos.

He pointed toward the boat, and Becks saw the Ranger pulling Cam toward the Defender, but he looked anything but okay, although at least he appeared to be conscious. Every fiber of her being wanted to go to Cam and help him, but as another mud-caked zombie was slithering out between a bookcase and a large advertising sign for "Express Lube," Becks had to take care of herself and the others first.

Pete was stretched out on his back across half of a dining room table, panting and clearly dazed. Max was stuck in the debris just a foot away from being completely submerged. Julian and Martha tried to help, but they could barely stay on their feet. Everyone had several hands and mouths threatening them from all over the garbage pile.

Becks heard the commander yelling for her to swim clear of the debris and head for the boat. She was about to protest, to say the others needed her help, when she saw that the boat was starting to nudge forward and put tension on a rope that appeared to be attached to the debris pile. Assessing the situation, she swam as fast as she could. A few seconds later, she heard an ungodly groaning and snapping sound, but didn't stop to look back.

With the deep, throaty roar of the Defender's two, 225-horsepower engines, the boat lurched forward, the grappling hook sunk deep into the heart of the pile, and the rope strained, but did not break. Suddenly, with a deafening crack, the tight mass of debris once again exploded into thousands of pieces of wood, metal, plastic, and flesh. Like tumbling dominoes, the four remaining team members were thrown into the water, churning head over heel and bumping and crashing into lawn furniture, picnic baskets, and zombies.

Julian grabbed onto Max, who was finally free, but it wasn't entirely clear who was helping who as they tried to swim toward the boat. Pete and Martha were both floundering. Pete, because he was so wounded, and Martha, not only because she had no idea how to swim, but she had never been in any water deeper than a bathtub, let alone a bathtub full of undead people trying to bite her.

The Ranger, who had gotten Cam onboard the boat, was about to dive back in after the others, but Tejada told him to stay, as he was too badly banged up. She pointed to two crew members, who each grabbed a life jacket and dove into the garbage-filled water. Within moments, both expert rescue swimmers had Pete and Martha in the life jackets and on their way back to the boat. After getting them safely onboard, both crewmen went back for Julian and Max.

Every muscle in Becks' body ached and burned, and in the last ten feet to the boat she felt as though she was never so completely exhausted in her life. Only after she had been yanked aboard like a rag doll with one hand by the Ranger, did Becks also realize she had half a dozen wounds, as well. She couldn't tell if they were bites or cuts from the debris, but it didn't matter, in this cesspool of rotten flesh they would all have to be treated for infections—both for ZIPs and the more prosaic, but no less deadly, varieties of bacteria.

Despite their injuries and fatigue, once on the boat, Becks and Julian began attending to everybody's wounds. Julian actually surprised Becks with his skill and efficiency, and for the first time since she met him, he didn't look scared. Damn, he *was* a doctor, and a good one!

Martha had bumps and bruises, and a few scrapes, but nothing serious. Pete was bitten and cut all over his body, but nothing life-threatening. However, given all he had been through the last few days, and his lack of sleep, he was in no condition to go on to Albany. That was a huge loss for the mission, especially given his knowledge of Project Decimation.

Max's right thigh was severely bitten, and it looked like his left ankle was broken. He would also be unable to continue to Albany.

Then there was Cam. Sweet, brave, ever-resourceful, handsome Cam, who now looked like a drowned rat; a rat who had been chewed up and spit out of a garbage disposal unit. Fortunately, the Defender had brought a supply of blood, and Becks worked feverishly to temporarily seal the major wounds so that the transfused blood didn't spill right back out. A medical team would be waiting at the dock at West Point to do the real work of patching him up. It was Becks' job to make sure Cam stayed alive until then.

"Are we good to go?" Tejada asked, after she gave the doctors a few minutes to assess their patients' conditions.

Just as Becks was about to say they could take off, and as fast as possible, Max pushed Julian aside and shouted, "No! Someone else is still out there! Someone is onshore, shooting, and he saved my life."

The Ranger started to disagree again, but Tejada interrupted and said that her crew had said the same thing. Someone on shore had shot the zombie that had attacked Cam and Becks.

"Get some eyes over there," Tejada shouted, as a couple of crew members grabbed large binoculars.

Only a few moments passed when one of the crewmen—a young man who looked like he should be in high school—yelled, "I got something! Over there, in a tree."

He pointed to a lone tree on shore to their south; a tree surrounded by hundreds of zombies.

"Can you see him?" Tejada asked.

"Uhhh … It's not a him, Ma'am," he replied, as a deep crimson blush transformed his pale skin into mottled blotches of embarrassment.

"A woman? Are you sure?" Tejada asked, grabbing the binoculars from the other crew member.

"As sure as I can be, Ma'am," he replied. "She's waving a pink bra in one hand, and her red shirt in the other."

Tejada focused in on the topless woman, who was sitting on a branch of a short maple tree. She had a rifle over one shoulder, and less than a yard beneath her feet were dozens of filthy, decaying hands reaching up, straining to grab her.

"Bring us around and prepare to fire. And get the grappling hook ready again," Tejada ordered.

Becks wanted to grab the wheel and head north at all possible speed, as every minute counted for Cam's life. However, this woman had saved *her* life, and Max's too, and they just couldn't leave her to die on Manhattan.

Max crawled to the side of the boat and asked for a pair of binoculars. With the ship speeding and bouncing around, it took some effort, but he finally managed to zero in on the woman in the tree.

"Son…of…a…*bitch*!" Max shouted, laughing, and then added with admiration and something suspiciously like affection. "It's Margo! She *is* too pig-headed to die!"

Pete and Martha were delighted by the news, and Max reminded the others that Margo had covered their retreat after they launched Pete on the raft, and that they thought she had been killed. Max never liked Margo before. In fact, they did nothing but argue, if they spoke at all. However, now two things worked in her favor in Max's eyes—she had saved his life, and she didn't look half bad without a shirt. Even in the zombie apocalypse, men still succumbed to the timeless spell of breasts.

The river was filled with the debris and bodies released by the grappling hook, which made maneuvering a bit tricky, but much of it just bounced off the gray, foam collar that surrounded the C-class Defender's hull. Becks was too busy working on Cam to notice the grappling hook's second successful attempt to free up the shoreline, so Margo could make it into the water—once the herd was cleared, somehow.

As busy as she was, stitching and gluing Cam back together (using some of Sticky Pete's special blend), Becks did wonder why the boat then turned to face the shore, which provided lousy angles to fire the two M240B machine guns on the port and starboard sides. What she hadn't noticed—and what was now music to her ears—was that there was an M2HB mounted near the bow. It was a .50 caliber beauty that was currently turning the herd beneath Margo's feet into a field of zombie hamburger meat. Becks missed her beloved .50 cal and she had to restrain herself from knocking aside the gunner and taking over!

It was dangerous business firing such a weapon so close to Margo, but they were all out of time and options, so the risk had to be taken. When the .50 cal went silent, Tejada got on the megaphone and told Margo to climb down and get to the river, which was more easily said than done, considering all the time she had spent up in a tree without food, with only rainwater to drink, and practically no sleep.

Tossing the bra and slipping the T-shirt back over her head, Margo slowly and carefully lowered herself to the ground. Her legs were so shaky she immediately fell into the mass of chewed up zombies, but struggled back to her feet and cautiously stepped on and over more pieces of meat, bones, and organs than she had even encountered on pig-slaughtering days. To Becks, it seemed like it took forever for Margo to finally reach the water, where the two rescue swimmers were waiting for her.

No one was more surprised than Margo, when Max crawled over to her and gave her a big hug—in her wet T-shirt. Julian immediately focused his attention on her, starting an IV and injecting any number of things. Fortunately, she had no serious wounds, but the physical, mental, and emotional stress of the last couple of days had left her in a seriously compromised condition.

"We'll take care of you, Margo," Max cooed, holding the bewildered woman's hand. "Don't you worry, I'm here for you."

The ride up the Hudson was a blur, literally and figuratively. The rain had intensified again, and at high speed it was like racing through solid sheets of water. Becks was trying to concentrate, and not think back to the desperate boat trip from Bannerman's Island to the Hudson-Athens lighthouse the day that Cam had been shot and needed life-saving surgery, but the smell of his blood kept bringing it all back to her. How much terror and heartache could they all keep taking?

After Julian had gotten Margo as stabilized as possible on a boat racing and bouncing up the river, he joined Becks in trying to staunch the flow of blood from Cam's numerous wounds. He spent a few moments with a puzzled expression digging around in a gash in Cam's back.

"Well, this certainly wasn't helping!" Julian exclaimed as he extracted a human incisor from the jagged wound. "I keep telling the zombies to brush their teeth or they'll lose them."

Becks stopped in mid-stitch to a slash on Cam's forearm and looked at Julian in surprise.

"Wait, was that just a joke!?" she asked, totally unprepared for something so uncharacteristic from Julian.

"It's called bedside manner," Cam whispered, speaking for the first time since they got him on the boat. "Maybe you could learn something from him, Miss Undertaker Face."

Sweeter words Cam could not have spoken to Becks. If he had the ability to make a snide remark, he still had some fight left in him, which increased his chance of survival.

"If you don't stop bleeding all over the deck, you're going to need an undertaker," Becks shot back, as Julian's eyes widened in alarm. Becks would explain to him later that the worst thing to do would be to act nice to Cam, because then he would start worrying.

As they were passing under the Tappan Zee Bridge, Becks thought back to the day she saw her first zombie; the day her world started to crumble. She missed her Nyack home, she missed her parents terribly, and she even missed working at Nyack Hospital and ParGenTech. It all seemed like a million years ago and now so little was left, but absolutely nothing would be left if this massive herd from Manhattan swept through the Hudson Valley.

Chapter 14

"We're fifteen minutes out," Tejada informed Becks and Julian after they had finally finished stabilizing Cam. "I suggest you two grab an MRE now, as we'll be shoving off again as soon as we offload the wounded and refuel."

Neither of them realized just how famished they were until the mention of food. Becks resisted the impulse to ask Julian if was going to throw up his meal again, and just concentrated on wolfing down her own food. The MRE also brought back unpleasant memories of being stranded in New Jersey, but she had to keep pushing all of those fears aside, as what lay ahead was frightening enough.

Medical teams at West Point sprang into action the instant they touched the dock. Becks just had a couple of seconds to say goodbye to Cam, who squeezed her hand tightly and whispered, "Go and do what you do best. Kick ass, baby!"

Phil was on the dock—and stuck out like a sore thumb, as he was the only one with an umbrella. He had a bundle of papers for Becks, and thankfully, a change of dry clothes.

"Heard it was rough out there. You okay?" Phil asked with genuine concern as he took hold of her shoulder

"Been better," she replied with a weak attempt at a smile. "Also been a lot worse."

Phil followed Becks into the triage tent, where medical teams acted like a pit crew stripping off her clothes and attending to all of her wounds. This was indeed a race—a race of life or death—and they needed to patch up Becks and Julian ASAP and get them back on mission.

"We put together some notes, and a list of equipment and chemicals that would be helpful," Phil said, standing behind a nurse who was stitching what looked like a bite wound in Becks' leg. "It's terrible that Pete can't go with you. Just terrible. But we have video coms set up and he should be able to monitor what you're looking at and let you know what to grab."

"But who will be with me, just Julian? He's less than useless in a fight," Becks whispered, as Julian was just on the other side of the tent having his minor cuts bandaged and treated for infection.

"Well, that's the thing," Phil hemmed and hawed, avoiding eye contact. "They can give you the other Ranger, but all other available personnel are needed in New Jersey and Rockland, setting up defenses and trying to thin the herd. It's bad down there. Really bad."

Albany won't be any vacation either, Becks thought to herself.

"There may be some locals at Albany who can help," Phil added, but without much confidence.

The MRE and a fresh set of clothes were the best medicine for Becks, and she took the bundle of papers from Phil and headed back to the Defender. There on the deck, standing all alone in the rain, was Martha. Everyone had forgotten about her, which was the story of her life.

"Go in the tent, they'll take care of you in there," Becks said, actually feeling kind of sorry for the pathetic figure of a woman.

"I will not get off of this boat," she stated like a stubborn toddler, as she crossed her arms for emphasis.

"Martha, we are headed up to Albany," Becks began calmly. "That's in the Red Zone. I don't know if you fully realize what that means. It's probably worse than what we just went through."

"I will not get off this boat," she repeated. "I know Project Decimation better than Pete. No one knew Dr. Devereaux's work better than me. I know all of the buildings at the college. I know the equipment. Maybe I can't fight like you, but *you* need *me*."

"I can't argue that you would be a great asset," Becks agreed, while thinking that on the other hand, now she and the Ranger would have two people to babysit, which increased everyone's chances of getting killed. "Just as long as you know what you're getting into."

As the one Ranger was being driven off in an ambulance, the other Ranger arrived, and honestly, Becks really couldn't tell the difference—it was one towering wall of muscle in exchange for another.

Julian reluctantly stepped back on board, awkwardly shifting his body beneath the combat gear that had been thrust upon him. Becks thought it was like putting a coat and shoes on a dog and watching him try to walk.

Tejada and her crew came back from a quick briefing on where they would be going and what to expect. Until the last moment when the engines roared to life and they pushed away from the dock, Becks secretly hoped that someone would rush over and tell them the weather was breaking and a helicopter would be able to deliver them right onto the roof of the nanotech buildings. No such luck.

For most of the ride upriver, Becks, Julian, and Martha were absorbed in the bundle of Phil's notes, and in making their own notes, lists, and maps of the locations of labs and storerooms. But Becks couldn't help but be distracted, however, as they passed Bannerman's Island, where an Army-supported river militia now inhabited the Truesdale Clinic buildings.

At Newburgh, her thoughts turned to Smokin and she wondered how he was doing back at Cam's compound. However, she specifically avoided looking at the Hudson-Athens lighthouse, as the memories of operating on Cam were still too painful. Becks could waste no mental or emotional energy on Memory Lane, while they were most likely headed straight for the Highway to Hell.

How were she and the Ranger going to fight through the seven or eight miles from the river to the college with Julian and Martha in tow? And once they were there, what—and who—would they find inside? They would have to get a vehicle at some point to transport all the equipment and supplies back to the boat, but were there any clear roads, or were they all clogged with abandoned cars and zombies? And what about the locals—were any still alive, and were they hostile?

The Ranger approached Becks after listening for an hour to her, Julian, and Martha discussing what equipment and supplies they needed. There had been some disagreement about what was the most useful, and easiest to transport.

"Look," he said, picking up one of their lists, "I don't know a laser diffraction particle size analyzer from a differential centrifugal sedimentation centrifuge, so let's keep it simple. No fancy terms, okay? You point to what you want, and I'll pick it up and carry it. Agreed?"

Becks couldn't help but laugh as she told the Ranger it sounded like a good plan, because it was exactly the kind of thing Cam would say. She was hoping they would get a call soon with an update on Cam's condition, but so far, the radio had been silent. If only Cam was with her, she would be a lot more confident they could actually pull this off.

When the radio finally did crackle with a transmission, it had nothing to do with Cam, but it was still great news—new coordinates of where to come ashore to meet with some people who would have vehicles waiting for them. This changed everything, both in terms of having some additional firepower, and not having to go on foot possibly for miles, until they found a car or truck they could start. Everyone was breathing easier, but no one was under any illusions that this wasn't going to be a suicide mission—and their second one of the day!

Cam's first conscious thought after surgery was that mankind had been capable of landing a man on the Moon, but they still couldn't make anesthesia that didn't make you want to puke. The next thing Cam did was turn his head to vomit on the floor of the recovery room.

He was then informed that his punctured and torn blood vessels had been repaired, his wounds closed, and the latest anti-infection protocols administered. And, if he was a good boy, got some rest, and did what he was told, he should be up and around in a few days. Otherwise, the staff would be happy to strap him to the bed. Apparently, someone had tipped off the staff that Cameron Everett could be a rather difficult patient.

Phil came to see him and was delighted to find that he was already anxious to get up, but while the spirit was willing, the exhausted and drugged body was weak. Phil promised to get word to Becks that Cam would be okay. There was something else Cam wanted to tell him, something about a call he had made that morning, but the drugs won out and Cam fell asleep in midsentence.

Chapter 15

Becks, Julian, and Martha needed sleep, too, after the strenuous and stressful hell they had been through that morning. Once their meeting was complete, the three curled up on the bouncing, rolling deck, and even with the loud rumble of the engines, were out in less than a minute. Hideous zombie faces, grasping hands, and biting teeth filled their dreams, but even those intense nightmares weren't enough to wake them. All too soon, however, Tejada's voice informed them once again they were "15 minutes out" and they should prepare to "hit the ground running."

As it was the Red Zone, the Defender would drop them on the riverbank and then have to move to a defensible position in case there were scavengers who would just love to get their hands on one of the fastest and most heavily armed boats on the Hudson. Modern pirates were making a good living with far less.

Everyone was on high alert as they approached the landing coordinates. No one knew anything about the people who were meeting them, so it made sense to arrive locked and loaded. However, Becks' sense of danger quickly melted into joy and amusement, as even at a couple of hundred yards, she recognized the shaggy, hulking figure standing on the hood of a Humvee waving to them.

"Stand down, stand down, it's okay," Becks shouted to the crew and the Ranger, who had already divided the dozen or so "targets" between them. "I know these people. Stand down!"

"Can you trust...*them*?" the Ranger asked dubiously, as the ragtag bunch of men and women came into clearer focus.

"With my life," Becks replied without hesitation.

As the Defender reached the riverbank, Becks leapt from the bow into the waiting arms of Charlie "The Monk" Ferguson. The Monk was Cam's right-hand man at the compound in Saugerties and had filled the leadership role since Cam had been at West Point with Becks. He was a former outlaw biker gang member, turned spiritual sage, and was also the man who had given Becks her tattoos, which she had actually grown to love.

The Monk's bear hug took her breath away, and she relished every second of it. The trajectories of their lives couldn't be more different, yet they had become fast friends who trusted each other implicitly. If Cam couldn't be with Becks, The Monk was the next best person to watch her back.

"What the hell are you doing here?" Becks asked, once she was able to catch her breath.

"Cam called this morning. Said you were getting yourself into more trouble," The Monk replied with a wink and a twinkle in his eye. "And you know there are two things I love most in this world—Dr. Rebecca Truesdale, and trouble!"

It had been a long time since the two had been together, and while she probably looked worse for wear, she was surprised to see her perpetually robust friend looking pale and a lot thinner.

"You on some sort of a spiritual cleansing diet?" Becks asked with concern.

"Just maintaining my girlish figure," The Monk replied waving it off with a smile. "Now let's get this show on the road!"

Becks said hello to the other half dozen members of the Saugerties compound she knew from the months she spent there, and was then introduced to other volunteers from Albany. She then introduced the Ranger, Julian, and Martha to them, and gave a quick briefing on the mission.

The Monk told her that the roads in the Red Zone were thick with debris, abandoned cars, and zombies, but they had "borrowed" three snowplows from the Albany County Highway Department. Driving in a staggered line across the road, they had cleared a path to the river by the intersection of highways 90 and 787. They planned to get on Interstate 90 and "plow" the seven miles to the campus of the Colleges of Nanoscale Science and Engineering. It might be slow going getting there, but once cleared it would be a breeze getting back to the river.

When The Monk got word from Cam about the Albany mission, he contacted the "Mayor of Albany," or so the locals had named him, a man known only as "Digger," who had taken it upon himself to bring some civilization back to the former capital of New York, which had collapsed into lawless chaos after quarantine.

The Army's push to clear the Hudson Valley had ended in the middle of Albany, which was now a slightly less lawless and chaotic frontier town surrounded on three sides by the Red Zone—where basically nothing but zombies roamed the streets. Digger had managed to create trading posts, clinics, and a police force of sorts. He even got a movie theater up and running so once a week the few inhabitants of Albany could get together and forget about the outside world for a couple of hours.

No one knew Albany better than Digger (and no one knew how he got his nickname, but decided not to ask) and when The Monk and his team arrived, it was Digger who brought them to the highway department's snow plows, and then led the way to the rendezvous point he suggested by the river. The Monk's team never would have made it to Becks in time without Digger's knowledge of the roads and the conditions around Albany, and she and the Ranger would have been on their own with Julian and Martha in tow.

"I thought you might want to drive this," The Monk said, tossing Becks a set of keys that were very familiar.

Becks had been so excited to see her old friend that she hadn't noticed that he had not just been standing on any Humvee, but *her* Humvee! It had been given to her by Sargent Pelton at West Point, and Becks and that vehicle—with her beloved .50 caliber machine gun—had been through hell and back together. She had given it to Cam when she started working at West Point, and she missed that deadly beast of a juggernaut.

She could knock down and run over a small pack of zombies like they were cardboard boxes. And the .50 cal, well, as Becks had recently been reminded by the Defender's .50 cal in New York City, it was capable of unleashing its full wrath on zombie bodies and turning them into exploding volcanoes of blood and guts, leaving nothing but lava-like puddles of remains.

"You always did know the way to my heart!" Becks said, giving him one more hug before gesturing to the Ranger, Julian, and Martha, that they were going with her, and that *she* was driving.

It was an interesting convoy as the three snowplows pulled onto the road, followed by two pickup trucks with "zombie catchers" welded to the front and mounts for automatic weapons along the sides. Becks and her dear Humvee took up the rear.

A few small herds of zombies were wandering along I-90 and were easily dispatched by the line of powerful plows. With a staggered, half-V formation, the bodies—or more accurately, body parts—of the smashed zombies would be shoveled off to the right side of the road. By the time

Becks drove over the cleared area, nothing but red blood and green fluid (from the ZIPs) streaks covered the highway, like some macabre Christmas parade.

Abandoned vehicles were a little trickier. The plows had to slow down and gently nudge the cars off to the side. Occasionally, an odd angle or something with flat tires required one of the plows to leave the formation and guide it off to the shoulder, but for the most part, the slanted formation was sufficient to clear a wide path down the highway. Though they were making good progress, there looked to be only a couple of hours of daylight left, and constant storms would make it even darker, faster. The last thing any of them wanted was to be inside the buildings in the dark with who-knows-what.

A bright flash of lightning up ahead suddenly reflected off the abundant glass of the college structures as if to announce their goal was near. Small talk had already been at a minimum during the ride, and now there was silence for the final mile as Becks and the team knew they were headed into yet another shit storm. No one had any intel on the area, and The Monk did not have enough advance notice to have scouted it out. They were just lucky they were able to clear the way to the river in time to meet Becks.

The entrance to the main parking lot was blocked by a line of cars which looked as though they had been placed there way back during quarantine. Becks wondered if, like at ParGenTech, the college had offered shelter to students and family members who wanted to continue their work—or who had no families to return to—during the "temporary" quarantine. That quarantine was supposed to save humanity, but instead, led to the complete collapse of civilization in the Hudson Valley, and eventually the entire country.

The snow plows tightened up their formation to almost a straight line as they pushed the string of vehicles out of the way. There weren't many other cars in the parking lot, and it certainly didn't look like anyone had been to this campus in a very long time. That was good, in that it probably meant that no large groups of scavengers or survivors were inside.

As for those who hadn't survived, during another lightning flash, Becks and a few others noticed a female zombie with her face and hands pressed against a third floor window in one of the buildings as they were passing by. There were probably many more with her, as zombies were like roaches—if you saw one, there were probably many more.

With the light fading, it was decided that the group would split up and go to separate buildings. Becks would be part of one team with Julian, The Monk, and several of his people, while the others would form the second team. Yes, there was strength in numbers, but every minute counted if Project Decimation was going to stand a chance. Digger would remain behind and guard the vehicles, in case there were any scavengers in the area.

There was just no way the massive New York City herd could be allowed to disperse throughout the Hudson Valley and Northern New Jersey. Everything they had all worked so hard to rebuild would be lost again. The military just didn't have the personnel and firepower to take out the entire herd. There was some talk about possibly using a small, tactical nuke, but that was the last resort, as the area didn't need radiation concerns on top of everything else. After all, it was the Fukushima radiation that initiated the zombie apocalypse in the first place. Becks was unaware that the top brass had put the nuclear option on the table, which was probably for the best, as she had more than enough to worry about at the moment.

The doors to both buildings were locked and groups of zombies in lab coats and Tyvek suits had gathered up against them, due to the noise and movement outside. Discussion about how best to enter the buildings and dispatch the zombies safely was rudely interrupted when Becks drove her Humvee in front of the entrance to the first building and squeezed off some glass and bone-shattering rounds from the .50 cal.

"There you go," Becks shouted to the two teams, unable to suppress a huge grin. "No doors, no zombies."

She then drove over to the second building and had even more fun, as the crowd of zombies she shredded there was even larger.

"That's my girl!" The Monk said and then kissed the top of her head and ruffled her hair when she rejoined the team. "Now let's go help save humanity… Again."

The Monk and his people moved like well–oiled machines, as they had the technique of clearing buildings down to a science. As they were looking for very specific items, doors that didn't need to be opened stayed closed. Fortunately, there were only a few stragglers here and there; once young, vibrant students pursuing groundbreaking research in what was still a relatively new science, who were now reduced to mindless, wandering corpses.

There was one Asian boy who stood out from the rest. As Becks dispatched him with her combat knife, she noticed he was wearing a T-shirt that read, "Nanotechnology: Size Matters." Normally, she would have laughed, except that this boy couldn't have been more than 19 when he switched, and she was now wiping bits of his brain and eye jelly off her blade onto that T-shirt.

She would never say this out loud—and certainly not in the present company—but it always hurt her more to kill zombies like this. Scientists, doctors, and engineers were the best and brightest who were supposed to lead the world to a better future for the next generation. Unfortunately, the ZIPs didn't know a brilliant brain from someone as dumb as a post. ZIPs were equal opportunity parasites. To them, the gray matter of DaVinci and a window washer were interchangeable.

There was little resistance finding the first lab they were looking for on the second floor. The Monk's people had thought to bring lightweight, folding shopping and luggage carts, and quickly began filling them as the two doctors pointed out what needed to be transported. The labs had been greatly expanded, and contained a lot of new equipment since Becks had been there. The video coms were sketchy, but they were able to contact Pete at West Point on two occasions to ask questions.

While the other people from Cam's compound did all the running back and forth to the vehicles to load everything, The Monk stuck to Becks like glue, from floor to floor and lab to lab.

"Cam told you not to let me out of your sight, didn't he?" Becks whispered when they were apart from the others for a moment.

"Why would Cam say that?" The Monk replied awkwardly.

For all of his abilities, and past criminal activities, he was a terrible liar. Becks was about to reply, when gunfire erupted at the end of the corridor. Dropping everything, they ran toward the far end of the long hallway and found two team members and Julian firing into a large pack of zombies. There were dozens of them, and no one knew where they came from, or how many more were on their way. They were dressed in lab gear, as well as maintenance and security uniforms, so they were from the college. They must have been in the cafeteria or an auditorium, and had been drawn out by the sounds.

"Get back," Becks shouted. "Take what you have and get the hell out of here!"

Becks pointed toward the other end of the corridor, and added that they had gotten most of what they needed and it wasn't worth risking it any further with so many zombies, and it was getting dark rapidly. Julian didn't need to be told twice to retreat, and Becks was surprised at just how fast he could run in all that combat gear, while carrying a big box of chemicals.

Becks raced back into the last lab she was in to grab a bag stuffed with supplies she had packed, and when she ran back into the corridor, she found The Monk doubled over on the floor, popping a few pills into the back of his throat.

"Monk! What happened!?" she yelled, searching him for wounds, wondering if he had been hit by a ricocheting bullet.

"Go on, Becks…Get out with the others," The Monk said between labored breaths, in obvious pain, as he pushed her away with one of his massive hands. "I just need a minute…I'll be right behind you."

"Like hell! I'm *not* leaving you," Becks stated with firm resolve. "And I don't think we have a minute. What's going on?"

The herd of former college students and employees had reached the top of the stairs and was making a beeline for them.

"Just a cramp," The Monk lied poorly again. "Now get your pretty ass out of here."

Becks didn't respond to him and instead got on the com and declared an emergency. She needed help carrying The Monk—a lot of help—and she needed it ASAP. Julian replied that they couldn't make it back, as they were cut off by another herd coming down the other stairwell. They had just gotten out in the nick of time. The Ranger also replied that his team had their own troubles—which was emphasized by Martha screeching obscenities in the background in between gunshots—and would need at least ten minutes to get there.

The herd to Becks' right was less than 100 feet away, and she just glimpsed the tops of the heads of the other herd to their left as they began descending the staircase to their floor. They didn't have enough ammunition to kill all the zombies, and there was no way Becks could single-handedly fight them off with her knife in such close quarters and in such dim light.

"Monk, for god's sake, what the fuck is going on? The truth! Now!" Becks shouted, trying to drag him into the lab. She would just have to barricade the door and hope the combined firepower of all the others could clear the corridor.

"The Big C," The Monk replied, wincing. "Pancreas, liver, you name it. Found out a couple of months ago. My concoction of pain pills had been helping, but not so much anymore."

Becks had no words, she just hugged him. But there would be plenty of time for sympathy later—now she had to get them to safety.

"No, stop!" The Monk protested, as Becks tried to pull him a few more feet. "You have to get out of here."

"Well, that isn't exactly an option right now," Becks replied, even though she would never consider leaving him behind even if she had a way out.

"Yes, it is," The Monk said, mustering all his remaining strength and energy to get to his feet and raise his automatic weapon, which he used to blast the glass out of one of the large windows.

"That's way too far to jump," Becks stated, glancing down to the concrete several stories below. The Monk pulled a bright yellow loop of rope from his belt and started wrapping one end around Becks' chest, and then under her arms.

She continued to argue, still not comprehending The Monk's plan, as she fired a few shots into the zombies who had drawn dangerously close on both sides. Then suddenly Becks felt everything spinning. The Monk had lifted her up sideways and was preparing to drop her head-first out the window. She yelled for him to stop, but he had already tied the other end of the rope around his waist and was determined to save her, at any cost.

Becks tried to grab the window frame, but it was too late, and she dropped ten feet before the rope yanked tight under her arms and she was jerked to a stop.

"Monk, no, pull me back!" she screamed. "Please, pull me back!"

In the flashes of lightning, she could see that several zombies had already reached him, but despite the onslaught of bite wounds he was now receiving across his body, The Monk held fast to the rope and began to lower her slowly and safely to the ground. Digger, Julian, and some of the others gathered below and aimed for The Monk's attackers, but no one had a clear shot as the zombies swarmed over him. Becks could hear The Monk shouting a string of profanities—until he started chanting something in a foreign language. Becks imagined it was some Tibetan death prayer, and tears and rainwater streamed down her cheeks.

Then the chanting stopped and she started dropping quickly. Bracing for impact, she stopped fifteen feet above the concrete. Grabbing her combat knife, she reached above her head and cut the rope–but only after holding onto that rope as if it was The Monk's hand, and sending a prayer to him through it. Digger caught Becks as she fell, and he asked if she wanted them all go in to try to help The Monk, but she just shook her head and whispered that it was too late, as she turned her back and walked away.

Becks didn't want to look back up to that window. She couldn't bear to see zombies slurping a tasty morsel of The Monk's flesh. She wanted to get the Humvee and pour lead into that section of the corridor and kill them all, but what would that accomplish?

The Monk's people were also devastated by the loss of their beloved leader and friend, and they all silently went back to the vehicles. The other team joined them in a few minutes, a little battered and bloodied, but all intact. No one asked any questions, as they understood what had happened.

On the long trip back, Becks decided she would be adding one more tattoo to her arm, one of an angel—a very large, shaggy-looking guardian angel.

Chapter 16

"Loneliness corrodes the soul," Joanna Gilchrest often thought, and she had a lot of time to think. She had lost her three young children in the early days of infection. Her husband had been killed by scavengers a few months after quarantine. Like the majority of other Americans, she had no idea what happened to her parents, two sisters, brother, and their families, and various other relatives and friends across the country. When the phone, Internet, and mail systems collapsed, our once tightly interconnected world instantly became one of isolation. No one could have prepared for, or imagined, how cruel that loneliness would be.

For a time, Joanna survived with the mutual cooperation of several neighbors. They made weapons to fight the zombies, scrounged for supplies, planted a garden, and generally went about their business as if they were the last people on earth. But Frank was a 57-year-old diabetic and when his medication ran out, so did his life. Felisha was bitten—not by zombies, but by a tiny tick, of all things. She developed a high fever, went into renal failure, and died at age 38. Lance broke his leg when a tree he was cutting down for firewood fell on him. Without proper medical attention, a blood clot cost him his life. Then there had been Evelyn and Edward, a typical suburban couple, who decided that a murder/suicide pact was the only way to end the constant horror.

So now it was just Joanna, somehow managing to stay alive in her home near the Palisades Interstate Parkway in New Jersey. She had no idea that civilization had begun to return to the Hudson Valley, but even if she had, she was so entrenched in her loneliness and misery, she probably wouldn't have made an effort to reconnect with a new community. She had lost so much—in fact, everything—that complete isolation was the only way she could cope. While alone, Joanna didn't have to react to anyone, explain herself, or justify her willing submission to hopelessness. It really wasn't living, but it wasn't death, either, and that had to count for something.

Now things had changed, however. As she sat in her favorite chair—the one her great-grandfather had made for her great-grandmother as a wedding present—and looked out through the slits of the boarded-up front window, she saw a sea of zombie faces passing by. There was someone in

91

a heavily soiled white lab coat who might have been a doctor, or had he been a butcher? There were women with long tangled masses of hair with leaves and sticks stuck in them. There were very tall zombies and very short zombies, fighting to see above their taller companions. There had to be a thousand of the undead creatures surrounding her home and she couldn't begin to comprehend why there were so many, and why now?

Had she actually died and gone to hell? Poking a steak knife into the back of her hand convinced Joanna that she was still very much alive, but a bigger question now loomed—did she want to continue living like this, unable to go outside? How long could she survive on her limited supplies? She had no more prayers for a god she had been convinced long ago did not exist. She couldn't remember the voices of her own children. She had no hope of, well, no hope of *anything*.

For the time being, though, she would sit in that family heirloom chair and stare at the massive herd as they knocked down her fences, trampled her gardens, and pressed against the sides of her house like a surge of water from a hurricane. It was a zombie storm for sure, and if they did manage to somehow get into her home, the question of her very existence would quickly resolve itself.

Word of The Monk's death reached West Point before Becks returned, sparing her having to break the news to Cam. It was a terrible blow. Cam cried like a baby and didn't care who saw him. In this one death, Cam had lost his best friend, a second father, his right-hand man, and his spiritual guide. As much as he loved Becks, body and soul, they were very different people and would never completely mesh like he and The Monk. A part of Cam died that day, too, and while his body would heal from its recent wounds, he knew his spirit would never recover from this loss.

Then there was the guilt factor, which sunk into him more painfully than a zombie's teeth. *He* had called The Monk and asked him to go on this mission. *He* had asked The Monk to watch over and protect Becks. *He* should have known that The Monk would look upon Cam's request as a sacred duty—one for which he would be willing to forfeit his life.

Even though The Monk had told Cam every time someone in the compound died on a mission that no one is to blame for such deaths, those words didn't really help him at those times, and they certainly didn't help him now.

The Monk had also said that for him, dying in a hospital bed would be worse than being eaten by zombies, but that wasn't any consolation either. Cam had no idea about The Monk's cancer, and how he literally gladly chose to go out heroically rather than die in bed, but even later after Cam learned about The Monk's condition from Becks, it wouldn't ease his grief. His only possible relief from his deep mourning would come from killing every fucking zombie he could get his hands on.

When the Defender arrived back at West Point, trucks and troops were there to transport everything they had collected at the College of Nanoscale Science and Engineering. Becks felt as if she was 90 years old as she climbed onto the dock. Phil was there to give her a hug, and fill her in on Cam's condition. Then he ordered her to go straight to her quarters to get some sleep, and was astounded when Becks didn't protest.

Julian and Martha were equally fried and no one would be of any use to the project until they were rested and clearheaded. Pete would oversee the setup of the new instruments and equipment throughout most of the night. Then it would be all hands on deck in the morning until Project Decimation could either be fully implemented, or they all became completely overrun like Joanna Gilchrest.

Becks dropped her wet, bloody clothes on the floor just inside the door to her room. As dog-tired as she was, she needed a long, hot shower. She couldn't prove it scientifically, but she believed that fear and grief created biochemicals that stuck to the skin like a "stink" of despair. She desperately needed to physically and mentally cleanse herself of the last couple of days.

Not until she stepped into the shower did she realize what a complete and total physical wreck she was. Her cuts and bites were red and swollen. Every muscle ached. She could barely lift her arms from all of the hand-to-hand fighting on the streets of New York City. Her feet were like throbbing blocks of lead from the mile after mile of running for her life. Her thighs and calves burned, and her hands felt as if someone had crushed them in a vice.

Worst of all, however, were the rope burns under her arms. But the pain was more emotional than physical, and when she closed her eyes she could clearly see The Monk's face for the last time, as she hung from that rope, her life literally in his strong, massive, but gentle hands.

After slipping into bed, she called the base hospital to get a message to Cam that she would see him in the morning. She told the nurse that she didn't want to disturb him from his sleep, but the truth was that she simply couldn't face him right now. Her emotions were too raw, and she also felt too much guilt. She had replayed the events over and over in her head and kept coming up with different endings—all of which resulted in The Monk still being alive, or so she managed to convince herself.

Sleep mercifully came quickly, and Becks was able to continue torturing herself with guilt in her nightmares. Everyone in the Saugerties compound who was able to sleep that night, also had nightmares. Many of them, too, felt guilt; especially those who now realized that the special kind of crazy and recklessness The Monk had recently exhibited was, in fact, part of his growing death wish—to die with his motorcycle boots on, so to speak.

Cam, Phil, Pete, Julian, Martha, Max, Margo, and the two Rangers certainly didn't sleep well either. No one at West Point rested well knowing what was coming.

Tremors of fear were reverberating throughout the entire Hudson Valley, and not since the early days of infection and post-quarantine did the entire population—or, what was now left of it—have such nightmares and terror about what the morning's light would bring. Even the Voice of the Hudson was back broadcasting again, urging all "you complacent sons of bitches to get off your asses and do something to save humanity."

"Begging your pardon, Sir, but this is a joke, right?" the nervous corporal asked the captain, who had just handed him two full pages of orders.

"Corporal, do I remind you of a comedian?" the captain shot back, his patience wearing thin from lack of sleep.

"No, Sir, you do not," the corporal responded crisply, automatically snapping to attention and aiming his eyes front and center to avoid the caustic countenance of his superior.

"Do I even look to you as if I am in the slightest bit of a good mood?" the captain continued, deciding to get some twisted satisfaction out of the moment.

"No, Sir, you most decidedly do not, Sir," the corporal replied, as if a drill sergeant was hammering him with questions.

"Then I trust you will now carry out those orders promptly, without any more questions about my emotional status, or the need for a punchline?" the captain added for good measure.

"This instant, Sir!" the corporal shouted, as he gladly ran off to round up everyone on the lists in his hand.

The captain really couldn't blame the corporal for his reaction to the unorthodox list of orders—they read like something from a bachelor or frat party. They were to scour through the roster of all the staff and civilians to find anyone who had been a masseuse, physical therapist, chiropractor, personal trainer, or physical education teacher. Anyone matching those qualifications was to be on constant call at the Project Decimation labs.

They also needed to find every doctor, nurse, and pharmacist, not already working on the project, and have at least two on duty at the lab at all times to dispense pain medications, amphetamines, or anti-anxiety medications as needed.

Food Services were to have a hot and cold buffet available at the lab 24-7, with both nutritional and comfort foods—and plenty, and more than plenty, of coffee and power drinks. And that was just the first page!

The second page of orders called for anyone at West Point who had any lab or technical experience of any sort. Even children with computer skills would be asked to pitch in.

And last, but certainly not least, were volunteers needed for the "Cowboys Squads"—the men and women who would be tasked with capturing—unharmed—the biggest and strongest zombies—with the best teeth—that they could find, and then corralling them in the sturdy pens the engineering corps was currently constructing on the parade grounds.

This was dangerous business, as the intense eradication campaign had effectively reduced the zombie population in the Hudson Valley to the occasional stragglers. The Cowboy Squads would have to go to the belly of the beast, into the jaws of the monster itself, to get the thousands of captives they would need for Project Decimation.

They would have to go down to the "Big Rotting Apple," as someone had dubbed the New York City herd heading their way.

Even with special body armor and protective gear, and armored vehicles with serious firepower, they might as well have called the groups Suicide Squads. Yet, of all the categories of people the corporal was tasked with rounding up, it was the Cowboy Squads that filled the fastest, to the point of being able to create four shifts of groups instead of only two, as originally specified.

The point of all this was simple: support the scientists working on Project Decimation in every way possible. If they were tired, pump them full of coffee and amphetamines to keep them on their feet. If they had a headache, give them a quick massage and painkillers. If they were losing their focus, take them outside for a round of yoga, calisthenics, or a jog. When they were hungry, offer them everything from a veggie burger with sprouts, to mac and cheese with extra cheese and bacon.

For those who were not working on the project, or supporting it in some way, there were plenty of other things to do, like arming and providing some very basic training to anyone from 10 to 90 who could stand and fight. And word was spreading even up into Canada, that if ever there was a turning point in the battle between the living and the dead, it was this one. If the Hudson Valley fell and was overrun, it might not come back again. The recovery of New England and New Jersey would also be in serious jeopardy.

A history teacher, who was now washing lab glassware, reminded everybody that in 1780, Benedict Arnold had tried to get the plans to West Point delivered to the British. The loss of such a strategic place in the Hudson Valley would have spelled doom for the patriots during the Revolutionary War. Zombies had now replaced the Redcoats, but the basic idea was still the same—losing control of this vital region would start the dominoes falling for humanity again, and this time, humanity may not recover.

In a similar vein, the elusive Voice of the Hudson spread the call for help paraphrasing Paine's "summer soldier and sunshine patriot" speech, with the addition of some very colorful vocabulary, of course. And he used just about every other appeal to their shared interests and honor-bound duty to the human race.

Apparently, his constant mix of cajoling and threatening began to work, to at least some degree, as a slow, but steady, flow of volunteers began arriving at the gates to West Point—and they came armed to the teeth. While almost everyone had to do something violent and awful to survive this long, few had the opportunity for some real payback to the ZIPs population on a grand scale, and they were ready to draw some zombie blood.

When the phone rang in Becks' quarters, her foggy brain thought for a moment that she was back in her parents' house in Nyack and all was right with the world. By the third ring, reality had set in, and the pain of The Monk's loss immediately resumed stabbing at her heart and conscience.

The call was to inform her that all Project Decimation personnel were being summoned to report for a briefing in one hour. That would give her time to dress, eat, and visit Cam. She wanted so much to see him, and know that he would be okay, but at the same time she dreaded it. She didn't know what she was going to say to him. After readying herself and going over in her mind what she would say for the tenth time, she took a deep breath, stepped into Cam's hospital room, and as soon as their eyes met, they both started crying. Becks climbed into bed with Cam and they wrapped their arms around one another and remained silent.

After several emotionally-charged minutes, Cam gently kissed Becks on the forehead and whispered, "Go now. Finish up what The Monk helped you start."

As Becks left the hospital and caught a ride to the lab, she thought about The Monk, her parents, and all of her friends and coworkers she lost at Nyack Hospital and ParGenTech. She also thought about all the people she had shot, stabbed, and burned—people who were just ordinary store clerks, accountants, customer service reps, pharmacists, and high school teachers BZA.

The ZIPs had not only killed and changed the victims they infected, they changed *everyone*. Some were changed for the better, rising to the challenge of survival against overwhelming odds. Unfortunately, however, too many sank to the level of their baser instincts and preyed upon strangers, as well as their former friends and neighbors. Those were the people Becks had killed, the ones who had been infected with hate, greed, and selfishness because of the ZIPs.

She was tired of all the fear and death, tired of always fighting. It was time to turn the tide of the ZIPs for good and eradicate every undead victim and every slimy zombie parasite on the face of the earth. Project

Decimation started today, and when it was finished, maybe the human race could come out of their dark shelters and walk in the sunshine again.

The lab was like an enormous beehive of activity. Becks wasn't exactly the queen bee, but she was part of the central brain trust that directed all operations for Project Decimation. In the lab itself, one group was tasked with creating the gold nanoparticles, while another group would synthesize Devereaux's pheromone-blocking compound that would be bound to the nanoparticles.

Then there was the treatment area, which was located in a gigantic tent, where captured zombies would be injected with the nanoparticles solution. This was tricky business, and required very special handling. It wouldn't be simple, like inoculating a herd of cattle. Ideally, the zombies should be flat on their stomachs, and the solution should be slowly injected into the spinal column. The treated zombies should then remain lying down for at least five to ten minutes for the best dispersal of nanoparticles throughout the body. Finally, after about six hours, a portion of the treated zombies needed to be "field tested," which basically involved putting them in a pen along with untreated zombies to see if they attacked them.

During the briefing, one of the colonels from West Point brought up a simple question that none of the Project Decimation scientists had considered.

"How will my soldiers know the difference between regular, untreated zombies, and a Project Decimation subject?" he asked, as Phil, Becks, and the others looked at one another and came up with a big, fat nothing.

Obviously PDZs (Project Decimation Zombies) were valuable assets, and once they were let loose on the "battlefield" so to speak, you didn't want them getting shot, unless absolutely necessary.

"May I then make a suggestion?" the colonel, a former military history professor at the academy, continued when he saw that no one had any idea what to do to make the PDZs stand out.

"During the Civil War, the local regiment of New York's Orange County men called themselves the Orange Blossoms. Granted, that name would not exactly strike fear in the enemy, but it does give me an idea. We have cases of fluorescent orange marking paint. Why not spray paint the hair and faces of the PDZs and create a new regiment of Orange Blossoms?"

Becks loved the idea and it was quickly and unanimously accepted. Work then commenced on the project at full speed ahead. The 72-hour goal was to have enough of Devereaux's solution prepared in the first 24 hours to begin injecting PDZs the next day. Row after row of treatment tables were being created in the tent, which included gurneys, conference tables, and even a couple of ping pong tables—anything horizontal to which a zombie could be strapped down to be injected.

If they could manage to treat about 30 zombies an hour for 48 hours that would give them close to 1,500 PDZs. That was just a fraction of Devereaux's calculated 1 to 10 ratio of treated zombie soldiers to the general population of zombies, but the first crop of Orange Blossoms might be sufficient to buy precious time to make more, and pray for human reinforcements across the Hudson Valley and from New England.

It had finally been decided to abandon the New Jersey suburbs campaign as large groups of zombies were found wandering away from the herd and heading west and south toward those suburbs. All of the troops involved, including Captain Lennox's special weapons division from the Picatinny Arsenal, would be forming a defensive line along the left flank of the massive herd. Their job would be to eliminate stragglers, try to keep the herd together, and thin it as much as possible without expending too much conventional ammunition. No branch of what was left of the military, or any militia group, had anticipated stockpiling millions of rounds of ammo for such a situation.

As stressful and exhausting as the various tasks of the Project Decimation teams were, no group worked harder or risked more than the Cowboys Squads. Legends were being made every hour by the exploits of the brave men and women clad in special body armor who drove straight down the Palisades Interstate Parkway, directly toward the herd.

Single zombies who were way ahead of the pack were scooped up first, literally, by front loaders that had been fitted to dump trucks. The biggest and strongest of the undead were shoveled up in the huge, industrial buckets, then raised over the cab of the trucks and dumped into the back, where mattresses had been spread out to minimize broken bones, as you didn't want to damage any potential Orange Blossom soldiers.

Unfortunately, in the first few hours these easy pickings were picked clean, and the Cowboys had to get closer and closer to the main herd. The sight of hundreds of thousands of zombies packed together—not to mention the sound and the odor—caused a few of the Cowboys to lose their nerve, but the vast majority stayed the course and went right up to the front of the enormous sea of zombies.

For the most part, they all stuck to the plan and tried to scoop up only those in the front lines that looked to be the strongest, but there were a few subjects that were worth the extra risk. For those zombies that were literally head and shoulders above the others, a Cowboy would hang out of the window of the truck and using a long pole, slip a snare around the zombie's neck or shoulders. Once the snare was secure, the truck shifted into reverse and plucked the subject right out of the crowd. After dragging him away a safe distance, they would release the snare and scoop him up with the bucket loader.

This was actually far more difficult and dangerous than it sounded. Instead of yanking the huge zombies out of the crowd, two Cowboys were pulled out of their trucks to horrific deaths at the hands—and filthy teeth—of the herd. Harnesses, such as those used in deep sea fishing, were soon installed to keep the Cowboys in the trucks.

On the flip side, sometimes as they were plucking out zombies they pulled a little too hard, resulting in several broken necks and the wasting of a good recruit. It took a few attempts before the driver and catcher refined their techniques, but by midday a steady stream of zombie-filled dump trucks were rumbling through the gates of West Point and emptying their cargoes into the special pens on the parade field.

The sight of these pens probably would have sent Phil into a flashback and panic attack, after his unimaginable ordeal at the Napanoch prison, so he made it a point of sticking to the lab to spare himself the possibility of the recurrence of those awful memories.

In truth, no one at West Point was particularly happy with hundreds of zombies pouring into their safe haven, especially as many had never been beyond the walls since the start of infection and had been completely shielded from the horror. But no one had much time to dwell on it, as everybody was so busy that there wasn't a moment in the day that wasn't filled with some sort of task.

Becks, Julian, Martha, Pete, Max, and Margo were the "go to" doctors and scientists who were personally going through all of the steps of the various processes to make Devereaux's solution. Each one had a group of four or five other doctors and scientists with them to teach them everything they needed to know. Each group rotated through all of the steps so that knowledge of how to produce the solution could then be spread to other locations—assuming anyone would be left alive.

Becks imagined that this is what wartime production had been like during the 1940s, with everyone pitching in and doing things they had never dreamed of doing. There was the former sanitation worker, who was now carefully weighing chemicals he couldn't pronounce for a process that he didn't understand, but he was so precise and efficient he quickly earned the nickname "The Measuring Man." A former kindergarten teacher was cutting leather jackets into strips, attaching buckles, and then screwing them securely to tables in the tent that would be used to strap down zombies and inject them. Half a dozen 10 to 15-year-olds were setting up highly detailed databases to track and collect information on all of the PDZs.

Becks' favorite story was of the 96-year-old World War II veteran who was instructing new recruits on the rifle range. Apparently, it was still quite obvious that he had been a drill instructor in the Marines and wasn't afraid to use highly colorful language to "motivate" recruits. It was also obvious that this was the best he had felt in decades.

While the *esprit de corps* at West Point was impressive, Becks didn't let it fool her into thinking that humanity was finally rising above all their petty differences. People were simply desperate, and they knew that if they didn't do everything they could to help make Project Decimation work, they would have to flee their homes and run for their lives—if there was anywhere safe left to run.

Despite the comradery, tensions were still running very high and arguments were widespread. A few fistfights had even broken out. Becks almost lost her cool a couple of times when one of the doctors she was teaching kept questioning and arguing about everything she did, even though he had absolutely no experience with nanoparticles and only a basic knowledge of parasites. Becks was about two minutes away from throat-punching him, when he suddenly burst into tears and apologized for his behavior. He explained that his wife and oldest son were on one of the

101

Cowboy Squads and he was so distraught and riddled with anxiety he couldn't think straight. At the end of his outburst, Becks actually gave him a hug!

Another unexpected problem arose within hours of the first group of treated PDZs being placed in their separate holding pen. Even though they were all gagged and had their hands tied behind their backs, they were still highly aggressive. Everyone was trying to attack everyone else, and they all ended up in a tangled pile of squirming and thrashing PDZs. This was an immediate problem as injuries and suffocations certainly would result, and every PDZ was a precious commodity. While this was a big problem at the present, it would be an even bigger problem when trying to transport them.

There was no way they could build 1,500 individual cages in a couple of days. Tying the PDZ's legs together would immobilize them, but then each subject would have to be carried. It was a little boy with a yo-yo who had "come to see the monsters" that gave one of the engineers an idea. Among the many things they had stockpiled were metal and plastic rolls of fencing, for farm animals, gardens, and for defensive purposes out in the field.

The engineer suggested tightly wrapping a PDZ in the fencing, pinning his arms to his side, but keeping him standing. Then like a jelly roll, wrap another two zombies facing outward from the center zombie, and then wrap in three more. This would make neat bunches of zombies who couldn't get at one another, but they could still be 'walked' to the trucks.

This "six-pack" idea was immediately tested, with acceptable results. PDZs could be rolled so tightly together that gags and ties for their hands could be removed. This would greatly simplify the dispersal of the PDZs on the battlefield, as a six-pack could be unrolled off the back of the truck down a ramp, keeping the Cowboy on the truck and not on the ground in greater danger. It would still be extremely dangerous work, but any edge would be welcomed.

After pulling a solid 24-hour shift, Becks was ordered to take off for eight hours. Normally, under such circumstances, she would have argued, but she was running on fumes and caffeine, and was beginning to feel as if she was going to shatter into a million pieces. She went straight from the lab to the hospital and was very relieved to find Cam sitting up in a chair eating solid food.

"You look like the one who should be in the hospital," he said, and meant it.

Making the mistake of glancing into the mirror, Becks had to agree. After giving him a five-minute briefing on what was going on, and a hug and kiss, she went to her quarters and didn't even stop to remove her shoes and clothes, and just fell backwards onto the bed. She dreamt of everything from tiny metal particles to massive herds of reanimated corpses, but at least she slept.

During Becks' downtime, the replacement teams who had been given crash courses in Devereaux's solution production began to take over from the original group, and were even able to expand production. Thanks to all of the equipment and chemicals Becks and the others had gotten from Albany, they were able to produce at least 50 times the volume of solution they would have been able to make with just what they had on hand at West Point, and what they had brought back from Columbia.

The Monk had not sacrificed his life in vain.

Six-packs of PDZs were being formed so quickly that it was rapidly becoming a logistical nightmare. It would take way too much time to load them all onto vehicles at once—if they could even scrounge up enough trucks and trailers—time that would allow the herd to overrun the communities of southern Rockland County. Commanders decided that transport would have to commence immediately and strategic drop-off sites would have to be found.

No one knew Rockland County like Becks, and when consulted, it didn't take her long to suggest Exit 5 of the Palisades Interstate Parkway. On the east side of the highway at Exit 5 was the site of a former drive-in movie theater, with a parking lot big enough to truck in scores of PDZ six-packs. On the west side of the highway had been a golf driving range, which also offered a big piece of open land to erect temporary holding pens for the PDZs about to be sent into battle. The exit also had a tactical advantage in that it was intersected by Route 303, which was currently zombie-free, and would offer access to additional troops, or as an escape route if things went south.

Becks recalled stories her father had told her about a huge World War II army base just a short distance from there in Orangeburg, called Camp

Shanks. Over a million soldiers from across the country were stationed there until they could be shipped overseas, and it came to be known as "Last Stop USA." Becks hoped these new camps would bring about the "Last Stop on Earth" for the massive herd of zombies headed their way.

Apparently, Becks wasn't the only one who knew local history, as when the first truckloads of Orange Blossoms were pulling into the former drive-in entrance, they saw that someone had hung a spray-painted sheet over the old theater sign that read "Camp Skanks." The name quickly spread and soon even the generals at West Point were calling it that.

When Becks got back to the lab, she found that production was moving along just fine without her. Even the newly-trained group of scientists and doctors were already teaching the techniques of making Devereaux's solution to lab techs, who were expected to be able to further increase production within 24 hours. In other words, Becks was already just another pair of hands in the lab—hands that at this point could be more useful firing guns.

"Becks, you've done enough. In fact, you've done much, much more than your fair share," Phil protested when Becks informed him that she was trading in her lab coat for the body armor of the volunteer troops. "Let the others take care of the actual fighting. You need to rest."

"Phil, could you just see me sitting in a lawn chair by the river with a good book and a cup of chamomile tea? We both know that's not who I am," Becks said, jotting down a few notes on procedural improvements she had thought about on the way to the lab. "You don't need me here now. What they desperately need are field commanders, especially ones familiar with the area. Recruits are piling in and without the right people to lead them they are just a disorganized mob."

"Sergeant Becks!" Phil said smiling, resigning himself to the inevitability of the situation. "I guess I always knew this day would come."

"Well, actually it's *Commander* Truesdale," Becks replied with a wink as she handed her notes to a project coordinator. "And I'm counting on you to hold down the fort and keep an eye on Cam."

"Speaking of Cam, have you told him yet?"

"On my way to see him now," Becks said, and then gave Phil a long hug.

"Maybe someday we can stop saying goodbye. Take care of yourself," Phil whispered, wiping away a tear before Becks could see it.

As Becks was leaving the lab building, she was surprised and pleased to be joined by Sticky Pete and Margo, who had also "enlisted" in the new army. Not in top shape, by any means, they were both nonetheless determined to stand and fight with everyone else. On their way to Combat Headquarters, a Humvee pulled up alongside of them and the driver asked if they needed a ride.

"Cam!?" a stunned Becks exclaimed. "What the hell do you think you're doing?"

"Good morning to you, too," Cam said laughing, but couldn't help wincing in pain from the movement.

"Get back to the hospital, you idiot!" Becks shouted.

"No can do, *Commander*," Cam said with that damned disarming charm. "I have been cleared for non-combat duty and assigned to be your driver."

"I'm sorry, please say that again," Becks said, turning from complete exasperation to amusement. "*You* have been assigned to *me*? *You* have to now take orders from *me*?"

"Yeah, just like it's always been from the day we were married," Cam replied and then dodged the notebook Becks threw at his head. The sudden movement made him wince again.

"Good for your stupid ass," Becks said, climbing into the front passenger seat. Pete and Margo hesitated, and then got into the back as they exchanged silent glances which indicated that the marriage info was news to them, but they weren't about to ask any questions!

Combat Headquarters was barely organized chaos in a manner that only the military could create. Information was streaming in from all over, and in any form of electronic communications they could cobble together, from modern satellite phones to Vietnam War-era radios. In the center of it all, a handful of officers were barking orders while standing around a large, 3-D, plaster relief map of the Hudson Valley.

The map had been removed from a tourist visitor center, and plastic army men and vehicles from a toy set were being used to mark the positions of troops. A cadet's collection of monster figures was piled up on the Palisades Interstate Parkway to indicate the latest position of the herd, which was getting dangerously close to the New York border. Small

105

superhero action figures with their heads painted orange were now being placed around Exit 5 to indicate that the Orange Blossoms were already being stockpiled.

Cam and the others were a little uncomfortable being in the presence of all the high-ranking Army brass, and he was surprised that Becks waltzed in like she owned the place. He knew it wasn't that she was overconfident or arrogant; it must just be that she had gone through so much hell surviving on her own for so long that rank and insignias meant squat to her. It didn't even enter Becks' mind now that she wasn't just as capable as any person alive to face any zombie—or human—threat.

"Becks, we missed you at the last poker game," some gazillion-star general said to her as she stepped up to the improvised battlefield map.

I guess that helps, too, Cam thought, as he wondered what other surprises were up Becks' sleeve.

Getting right down to business, the generals explained the dire situation with the plastic army men and action figures. Before they could finish, new information prompted a corporal with a limp to push the pile of little Creatures from the Black Lagoon, and Predators, and Mummies even further up the Parkway.

As he moved the figures with a bridge used for shooting pool in the officer's club, a wind-up Godzilla suddenly sprang to life, left the pack, and marched over the elevated palisades cliffs and fell onto the cracked blue paint of the Hudson River. Now on its side, the Godzilla figure continued to slide its legs back and forth, spinning in slow circles.

Embarrassed, the corporal struggled to shut off the rampaging classic Japanese monster, and finally just shoved it into his pants pocket, where it continued to wriggle for several minutes. While the corporal wanted to crawl into a hole somewhere, it was a needed moment of comic relief for everyone else. However, more news was painfully sobering.

This latest report was bad—the front of the herd was starting to fan out into the woods and side streets. Despite the Army having hastily reinstalled the barricades at some exit and entrance ramps, the long expanse of woods and the lack of guardrails was too inviting for the herd, which had been packed tight like sardines for so long. This was the worst-case scenario—the wider the herd spread out, the more difficult it would be to stop it.

"We have to start deploying the Orange Blossoms now!" Becks stated in a tone that sounded like she was in charge. "Start placing them along the flanks to try to keep the herd together."

There was some discussion amongst the generals and they agreed to start releasing the PDZs, but thought it was best to just drop them on the Parkway in front of the herd. Becks began to protest that they didn't have enough PDZs yet for a full frontal assault, but soon realized the best thing she could do was get her ass to the front lines with as many troops as possible and assess the situation from there. But before leaving, she at least got the generals to agree to disperse the PDZs on the flanks "if practicable."

The few hundred volunteers assigned to Becks would have been a godsend at just about any other point AZA, but now they seemed ridiculously inadequate in the face of such overwhelming numbers. As she stood up in front of the ragtag group of men and women, there was clearly fear in their eyes, but there was also that determined look of seasoned combat veterans. Everyone who stood there today had fought long and hard to make it this far, even the kids who were probably no more than 13 or 14, but had already been through so much in their young lives that they looked years older.

"Our hope is that the PDZs will do all our fighting for us. If not, then we have to be there to stop the herd from getting farther north. If you're from the Hudson Valley, I don't need to tell you what we have all sacrificed to start rebuilding our lives here. And my thanks go out to those of you I hear are from Connecticut, Vermont, Pennsylvania, and even Canada—"

"New Hampshire!" a small group shouted, cutting off Becks, "Live free or die!"

"Maine! Dirigo!" a few others yelled enthusiastically, and then had to explain that their Latin state motto meant "I lead."

"Rhode Island," one lone voice called out, and left it at that.

"The great Commonwealth of Massachusetts!" a few dozen people shouted, and then couldn't help adding, "Go Red Sox!"

Everyone laughed as the Massachusetts contingent pulled off their jackets to reveal Red Sox jerseys, and then in unison put on their bright red baseball caps. Numerous Yankee fans in the crowd then started booing, and good-natured ribbing ensued on both sides. Becks let them all have a few moments of levity, as she knew damn well it might be the last time any of them would laugh.

"Okay, okay, there will be plenty of time to fight amongst ourselves when the job is done," Becks said, as she was astonished how everyone immediately fell silent the instant she started speaking. "Now you all have been assigned one radio person per squad, and you need to stick by that person as they will be your lifeline if you need help."

Becks put her hand on the radio strapped on her left shoulder as she continued.

"I will be giving you instructions as necessary, so please keep the lines clear. You all know the rendezvous point on the Parkway and how to park your vehicles," she added, referring to the plan to have all of the cars and trucks parked single file, aimed north, with the keys inside, ready for a quick retreat if the herd began to overtake them.

"You all know what we are facing here," Becks said in her most serious tone. "We *can't* lose everything we fought for all these years. We just have to beat them. *We...have...to...kill...them...all!* Now let's get to it, and go kick some zombie ass!"

A shout came up from the crowd and Cam could see the expressions of admiration on the faces of the troops for their leader, Commander Truesdale. Each man, woman, and child felt fortunate to have her in charge, as people literally told stories around their campfires of her bravery and adventures.

Becks was basically oblivious to it all, and still couldn't quite understand the way people responded to her with such respect. In her mind, in many ways she was still the nurse and med student under the thumb of arrogant doctors and professors. The thought that she had been transformed into a leader of men was laughable, and a concept with which she would never be comfortable.

Cam was so impressed by what and who she had become, but he knew he would just be wasting his breath if he tried to tell her. When he thought back to the first time they met, it seemed like another lifetime as the shy, brilliant, almost awkward girl stole his heart at first sight. And now kick-ass Commander Truesdale in body armor and bristling with weapons was about to lead her troops into battle!

It often takes a crisis for someone to reach their true potential, Cam thought. *It's just too bad that this crisis had to be a zombie apocalypse!*

As Becks' convoy headed south, the Orange Blossom PDZs were rolling off the trucks along the front lines—literally. The Cowboy Squads were picking up a couple of six-packs of PDZs in the backs of trucks from the Exit 5 depots, then driving as close as they dared to the front of the herd, with orders to deploy the PDZs along the flanks, if practicable. While that sounded good on paper, the reality was that the woods along the PIP didn't allow for vehicles, so they had to drop off the Orange Blossom soldiers as far left and right of the herd as possible, and hope for the best.

As soon as the driver brought the truck to a halt, two more Cowboys would drop a ramp off the back. While they tried to walk the six-packs down the ramp, in their haste pushing the zombies along, the clumsy groups wrapped in fencing would usually fall over and roll down the ramps to the pavement. Once on the ground, the wire fasteners were cut and the six-packs were unrolled.

The next problem was to coax the PDZs to the herd, as their initial inclination was to immediately attack one another, or the Cowboys. Cattle prods and long sticks helped to break them apart and get them headed toward the herd, but it took time—too long to attempt these actions so close to the herd as the first squads attempted, as they were to tragically discover.

By the time the first two Cowboys had unloaded and redirected their PDZs, they found that they had gone too far from the truck and were quickly overwhelmed by the herd. The helpless driver looked on in horror as the two men were set upon, torn apart, and consumed like a school of piranha feasting on animals unlucky enough to fall into the water. It was a sight the driver would forever have seared into her memory, as the two Cowboys were her husband and brother.

The second truck had similar problems, but at least everyone was able to make it back into the vehicle before the herd surrounded them. They were trapped, but safe inside the truck, for now, although the sheer force of the unrelenting herd slowly pushed the big truck sideways along the pavement.

Orders and counter-orders shot back and forth across the airwaves as it was clear that the deployment strategy was unraveling faster than they could unravel the six-packs and get them where they needed to go. The third, fourth, fifth, and sixth Cowboy Squads had a little more success, but two more men were lost, and three of the six-packs were engulfed by the herd before they could be unwrapped. Becks listened to the chaos and confusion with increasing frustration and alarm.

Had all of their work been a waste? The trip to Columbia to see Devereaux, and running for their lives through the streets of New York City? Going to Albany for supplies and The Monk sacrificing his life? The hundreds of people working around the clock to make Project Decimation a success? Something had to be done, and done right now or the Hudson Valley would be lost.

"Stun the fuckers!" Becks shouted into her radio after she had dialed in the command frequency. "Stun the PDZs unconscious, unwrap them at the depot, and then use dump trucks to drop them *en masse* right into the front lines."

Cam took his eyes off the road long enough to look at Becks with a drop-jawed expression. There were probably a lot of jaws dropped at Combat HQ, as well, as for at least 30 seconds there was nothing but silence and static over the command frequency. Then the silence was broken, and by the familiar deep, booming voice of the commanding general himself.

"You heard Becks, stun the fuckers!" he yelled.

The depot personnel quickly responded with "Yes, Sirs" and Deployment Plan B was immediately undertaken, and with relish. The only thing more satisfying than putting a bullet in a zombie's head was to jam a stun rod into its ribcage and watch it twitch until it hit the ground. Timing would be tight, but thankfully most of the PDZs would remain unconscious until they could be driven the ever-shortening distance from Exit 5 to the front of the herd.

Becks' convoy was about ten minutes out as the first four trucks loaded with stunned PDZs were being dumped out of the backs of the trucks within a few feet of the front line. The trucks slowly pulled forward as their backs raised so there would be more of a line than one big pile of the bright orange-haired zombie soldiers as the trucks emptied their loads and raced back to get more. Observers reported what was happening, and unfortunately, about 10-15% of the PDZs did not regain consciousness in time to avoid being trampled by the herd. Another 20% began attacking along the front line, but their orange heads were quickly swallowed up into the sea of undead humanity. However, while forward progress of the herd didn't appear to be slowed, it was another story along the flanks.

It's easier to try to pass along the sides of an oncoming crowd than go up the middle, and the majority of PDZs naturally started filtering down the edges. The observers then sent up some drones, and in a very short time a thin, orange line was beginning to form along both sides, which hopefully would hold the herd together. This action was helped even further because when a PDZ would kill one of the herds' zombies, its ravenous companions would also stop to feed on the victim. It was only a drop in the bucket with hundreds of thousands of the undead still surging forward, but every zombie death and delay helped.

What also helped were the New Jersey troops, led by Captain Lennox, beginning their assault on the western edge of the herd. Again, with every zombie they killed, several more would stop to feed. While it seemed like they were trying to cut down a mighty oak with a penknife, if it prevented New Jersey from becoming an even more heavily infested hellhole, it was worth every bullet, arrow, and homemade spear.

Becks tuned in briefly to hear what was going on along the "Western Front," as Combat HQ was calling it, and all was certainly not quiet. From what she could glean from all the chatter, a large, local militia was fighting side-by-side with Captain Lennox and the Army regulars. She thought she heard that the militia was being led by a General Eddie, and a thrill of hope shot through her that it might be Big Eddie from New Ridgelawn, but she couldn't listen for too long, as her convoy was approaching the rendezvous point.

The closer they got, the more cars and trucks there seemed to be in their convoy. Becks thought she saw a few vehicles join them at the Palisades Interstate Parkway entrance in New City, and then more in Nanuet, Pearl River, and Orangeburg. Word of the herd had spread like wildfire amongst local residents, and while Rockland County was in imminent danger, people in Orange and Ulster counties knew that if Rockland fell, they would be next. The Voice of the Hudson was whipping everyone into a frenzy and more volunteers were also converging on West Point by land and river.

The convoy rendezvous point was supposed to be a mile ahead of the herd, but it was now less than half that, if they were lucky, as the terrible mass of zombies was clearly in sight, like a black fog on the horizon.

More than one person had to run into the woods to vomit as the awful spectacle—and even more awful smell—was just too much for their nerves.

Becks used a megaphone to get everyone to line up, and then quickly had the additional hundred or so new recruits, who had met them along the way, split up and join a squad. She gave a special welcome to some familiar faces, like Brian from Fort Ace in Ellenville, who had brought down a dozen fighters and some of their cool homemade weapons, and Digger, who had brought some of the Albany men and women and four of those powerful snowplows. And despite the seriousness of the situation, Becks also had to ask the young man who had arrived in an old ice cream truck what that was all about.

"My granddad was a veteran of D-day, and after the war he drove that ice cream truck around Pearl River. I figured if it was good enough for him, then I would be proud to drive it into battle."

It was clear by the faces of the older troops before her, that many of them had fond memories of those ice cream trucks on a hot summer's day. It had been a good life, growing up in the Hudson Valley, and it was now Becks' job to help make sure that future generations would also have the opportunity to make their own good memories here, as well.

Several more dump trucks with their cargo of PDZs passed them on their way to the front and volunteer troops cheered the Cowboy Squads for their bravery. By the time this latest batch reached the herd, no zombies with orange hair could be seen. Either they had filtered down the sides, gotten trampled, or were now deep into the advancing mass. Whatever the case, the herd continued to move forward. If it reached Exit 5, it could overrun the depots and spread north and south on Route 303. Once they began pouring onto the local streets and into the towns, it would be like the start of infection all over again, and nowhere would be safe.

Becks divided her little army into four groups, and appointed Sticky Pete, Margot, Brian, and Digger as group captains. As tempted as she was to use terms like "Red Leader," she kept it simple and called them by their first names. Throughout this brief process, Cam was looking increasingly anxious, shifting his weight back and forth and appearing like he was going to bust all of his stitches.

"Trues, you seriously can't expect me to stay out of this fight," he said pulling her aside as the troops geared up and checked their weapons.

"That's exactly what I expect," she said as a commander, with no hint of their close bond. "You shouldn't even be out of the hospital. You can barely walk, and you sure as hell can't fight. I can't be worrying about saving your ass every two minutes when I'm going to be responsible for all of these lives."

"But--"

"Aren't you the one who always says that everything after 'but' is bullshit? Now is not the time for you to be selfish. Think of everyone else. Stay with the vehicles and be ready to extract anyone who calls for help. Are we clear?"

Cam knew he couldn't have it both ways—he couldn't admire Becks for the leader she had become, and then ignore her when she made a wise command decision. He was still in rough shape, held together with sutures and bandages, and he would be risking others' lives by putting himself in harm's way in such a vulnerable condition.

"Yes, *Commander*. Understood," Cam responded with a salute of respect. "And permission to hug the commanding officer in front of the troops?"

"I would have you court martialed if you didn't," Becks said, falling into his open arms and trying to imprint every second in case it was their last moment together.

Taking a deep breath, Becks pulled away. Blowing a whistle twice, she then raised her right hand and motioned their advance toward the herd. It suddenly became very quiet as the hundreds of volunteer soldiers started walking toward the hundreds of thousands of zombies. The plan was simple—provide cover for the Cowboy Squads and do whatever they could to stop, or at least slow down, the herd

While she wouldn't openly admit it, Becks got the idea for her battle formation from old World War II movies she used to watch with her dad. In those movies, she saw that troops used to march behind the tanks for cover. While they were fresh out of tanks, they did have Digger's snowplows.

Splitting her forces between the north and southbound sides of the PIP, she had two plows, side-by-side, leading the way with squads lined up behind them in two columns on either side of the trucks. At first glance, they looked quite formidable, even given the dirty, undernourished individuals who comprised the majority of her fighting forces. As they drew closer, however, and the enormous juggernaut of the herd began to resolve into countless, sunken-cheeked corpses with their green and black teeth bared, it looked like more of a foolish and pointless suicide mission with every step.

The smell was indescribable and a steady stream of volunteers had to momentarily break rank to throw up, or have the dry heaves in the cases of those who had already vomited so many times that nothing was left in their stomachs. Becks fought hard to suppress the gag reflex as she didn't think it would be very inspiring to the troops if she bent over and hurled her breakfast.

The sound was also something for which one could never prepare. Becks thought it sounded something like a huge stadium full of people groaning in unison over a bad play by the home team. But there was something more to it than that—a sinister overtone that created the impression of very angry, and very hungry, wild animals.

A chill ran up Becks' spine and the hair stood up on the back of her neck as the faint sound grew to a loud roar. It might be difficult to hear over the radios with all that noise, so Becks personally jogged along the lines of the columns to pick young, healthy-looking runners to task them with spreading orders in case radio communications became useless. The designated runners joined Becks at the front of the farthest right-hand plow.

The formation on the left-hand side, marching south in the former northbound lanes, had to shift temporarily to allow several more truckloads of PDZs to pass, but there was no cheering this time. From where the volunteer troops on the ground were now looking, it appeared to be a lot safer inside those dump trucks, even if they were driving right up to the front line.

Combat HQ checked in with Becks to inform her that the supply of PDZs was already running low. If the zombie soldiers didn't start having some effect soon, the project would be a failure. And that was the good news. The bad news was to confirm that they would soon be in firing range and the new orders had her moving even closer to the front lines.

Becks imagined that corporal at HQ standing by the big Hudson Valley map pushing ahead a little group of plastic toy army men that represented her troops. She was secretly hoping the corporal had chosen some hot, female, superhero action figure to represent her, but the sound of distant gunfire snapped her out of her musings.

It was a comforting sound to know that Lennox and his army were peppering the Western Front with everything they had, but Becks was not under any illusions that they would be able to make a serious dent in the herd. With every passing moment, the desperation of the situation escalated. Had everyone at West Point, including her, completely underestimated the immense size and power of the herd? It just didn't seem humanly possible to stop this mass killing machine from obliterating the Hudson Valley. Still, there was more than one way to combat a seemingly overwhelming force...

Becks' mind now kicked into overdrive and an idea began to take shape. She had a different mental gear than average people, something that helped her concentrate, focus, and act at a higher level in times of extreme stress. It was something she had started to develop as an ER nurse, when people so badly injured or gravely ill had mere moments to live, and she and the doctors and other staff had to work together and do absolutely everything quickly and correctly, or it would be a fatal failure.

It was also something she experienced when Cam had been shot and she had to race up the river to the Hudson-Athens lighthouse to perform surgery—her first surgery on her own. She still vividly recalled the distinct smell of his blood, and the way the surgical gloves clung to her fingers, and just the right amount of pressure she had to apply to cut Cam's flesh to find the bullet—not too much to cut too deeply and cause more damage, but just enough to do the job.

That's what she needed now—not too heavy a hand that she marched her troops into certain death, but not so little action that it had no appreciable effect.

"Margo," Becks called into the radio. "Get up here ASAP. And all groups, send up some of your best marksmen."

Margo and about 30 others reported to their commander within a couple of minutes. Becks told them to double-time to within a close, yet safe, range where they would be certain to take down a member of the herd and not any PDZs.

"Head shots only, if you can do it," Becks continued, as Margo shot her a glance to the effect that there wouldn't be any question about her deadly accuracy. "I want as many brains splattering as possible. We have seen that when a PDZ takes out a zombie, it makes half a dozen others stop to feed. Take out as many in the front lines as possible, but for god's sake, fall back if they get too close."

As Margo and her marksmen ran toward the herd, Becks called Combat HQ with a new request. As the plan continued to form in her head, she realized that a lot would have to go correctly for it to work. Otherwise, it would be a fatal failure on an apocalyptic scale.

"HQ, I need eyes on the herd," Becks continued, as if she was a seasoned veteran. "I need to know where the PDZs are exactly, and if there is any change at all in the movement of the herd."

As she waited for a response, she could see the marksmen frighteningly close to the herd. Margo had them form two lines, one kneeling and one standing, with the shooters about five feet apart, and then had only one line fire at a time. Ammunition was precious, and a zombie only needed one bullet to the skull, not two or three. And they certainly didn't want to bunch up the kills. By spacing apart the shooters and controlling the pacing and rate of fire, Margo was ensuring the most efficient kills and spreading out the brains to attract as many hungry herd members as possible to disrupt the front line. Not bad for a med student, she thought.

The marksmen lived up to their claims, and skulls were popping open up and down the front lines. The irresistible aroma and sight of fresh brains was too great a temptation and a dozen zombies would drop to their knees in unison fighting over the tiniest morsel. Once they had sucked up every juicy, green slime-coated bits of brain, they plunged their teeth into the rest of the corpse, as if they hadn't eaten in months, which was probably actually the case for many of them.

After a few rounds of firing, Margo shifted the marksman on down the line and repeated the process until the entire front had bodies and feeders along it. Of course, by the time they had made it the length of the line, the herd had pushed forward and trampled and engulfed all of those on the ground, or at least that's how it appeared. Margo reported this to Becks who did not appear disappointed at all and just told Margo to continue firing up and down along the front line for as long as they could.

Becks and her troops on the southbound lanes had to move right to let more Cowboy Squad trucks pass. This time, as per her request, all of the PDZs were to be released along the front of the herd on the southbound side. It was one thing to hear about the PDZ drops over the radio; it was quite another to see it actually happening and even Becks stopped in her tracks for a moment as they watched the process.

The trucks rumbled toward the front line in single file, and then stopped just a few hundred feet away. Then, one at a time, the first truck pulled ahead until the herd was almost close enough to touch, and then the driver made a sharp U-turn—or as sharp as you could manage in a cumbersome dump truck on a two-lane roadway. If a few members of the herd got crushed and smashed in the process, so much the better.

As soon as the back of the truck was facing the herd, the bed slowly began to rise and PDZs started sliding out. Slowly moving forward, the mixture of unconscious and semi-conscious, orange-haired soldiers were spread out across the road. Unlike the problems encountered with the fully conscious six-pack PDZs, which immediately began attacking one another, the recently stunned zombie soldiers were attracted to all of the noise and movement of the herd, and for the most part, walked right past their fellow PDZs, who were still prone or struggling to get to their feet.

Once the first truck was empty, it sped back to the depot to refill, if there were any PDZs left, while the next truck in line followed the same maneuvers, trying not to run over any zombies with bright orange hair.

Becks anxiously awaited word from HQ about what the observers were seeing. She had almost caught up to the marksmen by the time some initial reports were coming in, and rather than have anything lost in relaying the information, the observers were patched into the HQ transmission, but all of them began talking at once and it took a moment until a single spokesman emerged.

"There is some commotion along the front lines just a few yards in, and there are certainly more swirls of orange," a very young man who only identified himself as Henry, began. Becks wondered if the boy was even more than 12 or 13 years old. But who better to fly the quad copter drones?

"Henry, Commander Truesdale here," she said dropping the army tone and speaking like he was just a neighborhood kid. "Could you explain to me in more detail what you mean by that?"

"Oh, hey cool, Hi!" Henry replied somewhat tongue-tied, clearly excited to be talking to the woman he had heard stories about around those campfires. "You know those orange-headed PDZs are showing up real

117

good and there's more and more pockets of them forming deeper into the herd. You know what I mean?"

"Yes, I do, Henry. What did you mean about the 'swirls' you mentioned?"

"Oh yeah, that," Henry responded quickly. "It's really awesome the way the orange is like swirling and spiraling. Ya know?"

"Turbulence! Yes!" Becks practically shouted as if she had just heard the best news of her life.

She thought back to a lecture she attended on fluid dynamics where the professor hated turbulence so much he was like a priest talking about the devil. To him, smooth, laminar flow represented everything good in the universe, and turbulence was an evil that must be stamped out, a disruptive force that brought chaos to the world. At this moment, however, a little turbulence would seem heaven-sent.

Regaining control, she then calmly and slowly spoke her next words. "Henry, I want you to take your time and look very carefully. Around those swirling orange pockets, is the herd changing direction at all, or doing *anything* different?"

"Uh, uh, let me see. Give me a sec," Henry almost whispered, as he deftly maneuvered his quad copter from side to side, and forward and back, as his other preteen companions managed their drones just as skillfully. "One more sec."

"Take your time, this is extremely important."

"Yeah, okay, it looks like around the orange swirls some of the zombies are trying to go off in different directions, you know? But most of them are just…well…uh…just stopping."

"Henry, please repeat that last thing you said," Becks requested as she felt her heart beating even faster.

"Yeah, sure. Around the orange swirls the zombies seem to be stopping, like hanging around like they aren't sure where to go. And we're checking the Western Front now, hang on, it looks like they may be stopping along there, too, 'cause between the orange heads and the army guys mowing down the herd zombies, they are making like a line of a big buffet of bodies and zombies eating."

"Becks, what does all this mean?" the commanding general finally asked, obviously out of patience. "What are you thinking?"

"Godzilla!" she replied with complete sincerity and confidence.

Chapter 17

At the moment Becks shouted, "Godzilla," only one other person on the planet had a clue as to what she was talking about. That person was not Cam, or Margo, or Sticky Pete, and it sure as hell wasn't any of the generals at West Point, who suddenly wondered if they had put a lunatic in charge of the volunteer troops.

No, the only other person was the corporal in charge of the Hudson Valley battle map, who immediately lit up with an expression of surprise and glee as he quickly hobbled over to the map.

"Can it be done? Can it possibly be done?" the corporal asked with great excitement to no one in particular, and everyone at once.

"Has *everybody* lost their minds?" the commanding general bellowed. "Will someone please tell me what the hell is going on!?"

"General, I think I have a plan," Becks began, but then made the general wait while she ordered the four squads to fan out across the highway to continue to do what Margo and her marksmen had started. "Remember when the corporal was moving all of those plastic figures across the Hudson Valley map this morning?"

"C'mon Becks, get to the point, we don't have time for—Godzilla!" the general said, as the light finally dawned. "Like zombie lemmings! But can you get the entire herd to turn?"

At that morning's briefing at West Point, a little Godzilla wind-up figure had activated and marched itself right off the cliffs of the palisades. As Becks faced the massive herd, the image of that little monster figure plunging over the steep, rocky precipice expanded like a giant movie screen playing over and over in her mind's eye. If they didn't have the personnel and firepower to stop and kill the herd, maybe they could get the herd to destroy itself by redirecting it toward the cliffs.

"I don't know if we can turn the entire herd, but even if we can get a good chunk of them to start moving toward the cliffs, it could make all the difference in the world."

"What do you need?" the general asked, hoping against hope her plan had a chance.

"Well, I don't know about Captain Lennox, but we could use more of everything here—more PDZs, more troops, ammo, some heavy-duty vehicles," Becks said as if she was ordering groceries.

"The last load of PDZs will be there shortly, and we have directed every volunteer who shows up at the gates to head straight to your location."

"You got any boats?" Becks asked, literally crossing her fingers.

"Plenty, but we can drive the volunteers there faster," the general stated, and then figured he had better look to his staff to make sure they nodded their heads in agreement, which to his satisfaction, they did.

"No, I need the boats to come down the river and make a hell of a lot of noise near the steepest, deadliest section of cliff you can find!"

"Roger that! Give 'em hell, Becks!" the general said, and then began spewing a remarkable, nonstop series of orders to just about everyone, twice.

The corporal carefully studied his map and found a deadly section of the palisades that would be the perfect "jumping off point," so to speak, and relayed the coordinates to Becks and Lennox. For Lennox and his men, the target section of cliff was due east. For Becks, she needed to head south and east, but in either case, it wasn't very far. Becks then asked Henry what the terrain between the herd and the cliff was like, and after a few minutes she heard that it was mostly trees, a few small roads, and a couple of houses, but no walls or fences that would impede the herd. A runner was sent to get a hastily drawn map from Henry.

Calling her four captains together, she devised a plan to keep Margo and Sticky Pete's divisions stretched out along the front line to continue inflicting catastrophic brain injuries on the zombie swarm. Any additional volunteers that arrived would also be put to the task. The other two divisions would head east through the woods and try to start drawing the herd in that direction. The snowplows would then form a moving wall to protect the troops where they could, but if the herd headed directly for them, as they'd seen before, even the heavy trucks would be useless.

Becks made a general announcement that they needed air horns, whistles, boom boxes, anything to make noise, and lots of it. As soon as the runner returned with Henry's map, Becks started to head directly into the woods to make their way to an access road that led south, and hopefully was currently relatively clear of zombies. Before she got more than a dozen steps, however, a strange sound filled the air, faintly noticeable even over all of the gunfire, groaning, and shouting that was echoing for miles around. There was something about this sound that seemed to somehow penetrate through all of the other noise and interference. Something oddly familiar, almost primal…

It must have been drawing nearer, as the sound grew in intensity and became unmistakable, causing both divisions to stop in their tracks, and the other two divisions to cease firing.

"That has to be Cam!" Becks said, shaking her head, wondering what that lovable dope was up to now.

From across the median of the PIP came Cam tooling along in the ice cream truck, headed straight for Becks, with that catchy, music box-like song blaring at full volume. Backtracking to meet him on the road, Becks had no words; she simply raised both arms in the air in *WTF!* exasperation. Cam turned off the music before he spoke.

"Hey, babe. I mean, *Commander* Babe," he began, but quickly stopped the facetious tone when he saw one of Becks' eyebrows raise. He knew from experience that meant she was moments away from DEFCON 1 status and was about to go nuclear on his ass. "So anyway, remember those videos of the zombies dancing and how they reacted to music? And remember that study that the Russian guy did with music that made the zombies cry?"

The vague, but accurate, scientific references got Becks thinking and the eyebrow returned to DEFCON 3; still dangerous, but she would at least listen.

"Go on."

"Well, I heard you call for things to draw the herd's attention, and what kid growing up in New York didn't gravitate toward the ice cream truck song?" Cam finished and then watched as both of Becks' eyebrows now furrowed into a deep thought line between her eyes, as she was transformed from Commander Truesdale into Dr. Truesdale in a heartbeat. She remained silent for several moments before she finally spoke in that researcher/physician persona.

"So, your supposition is that the familiarity of the ubiquitous ice cream jingle will engender activity in the medial pre-frontal cortex of the herd members, and draw them like a magnet, based upon fond childhood memories being enlivened by the biochemical interaction with the ZIPs' network in that region of the brain?" Becks asked in all seriousness, getting "lost in her science" as her parents used to say.

"Exactly!" Cam chimed in, not having a clue, but going with it.

"Brilliant!" Becks replied, leaning forward to give Cam a hug.

Becks then hopped in the passenger seat and directed Cam to the front of the column. It was rough going in an ice cream truck that was not exactly built for off-roading, but as it was also constructed to survive the daily onslaught of hordes of little kids, it held up just fine.

When Henry confirmed that they had gone far enough south on the access road that they were now behind the leading edge of the herd, Becks cranked up the ice cream music and ordered her troops to start making a racket. Tense minutes passed without any change of movement to report, so Becks asked Combat Headquarters to order a temporary cease fire, so that the only noise—other than from the herd—would be from her troops and that cloying, repetitive ice cream song.

It took a couple of minutes for all of the shooting to stop, but once it did, even Lennox and his men on the Western Front could hear the tinkling strains of the happy tune. Suddenly, everyone was thinking back to their favorite ice cream treat and how they used to run down the street after the trucks, clutching their nickels and dimes.

A minute passed as if it was an hour. Two more minutes crept by and Becks wanted to scream with all of her pent-up anxiety, and the incessant ice cream music ringing in her ears. Cam gripped her arm and mouthed the word, "Patience," and nodded his head with confident assurance, but she couldn't stand it much longer and soon asked Henry for a "sit rep."

"Well, it's just a few so far," Henry reported with no further explanation after taking at least five minutes to respond.

"A few so far, *what*?" Beck shouted, starting to lose her cool.

"Oh, yeah, sorry. I mean just a few zombies have turned and are leaving the herd and coming your way. But, ya know, when I say a few, you know I mean a few hundred, right?" Henry concluded, feeling satisfied as though he had just delivered a comprehensive report, but then remembering there was something else he wanted to add. "Ya know, you ought to drive down a ways and maybe start pulling some of the back end of the herd your way, too."

This was real music to Becks ears, as it meant that at least some of the herd had turned!

"Henry, I need you and all of the observers to watch this herd like a hawk. If a zombie so much as sneezes, let me know!"

"Do zombies sneeze?" Henry asked like the inquisitive child he was, but after one of his friends elbowed him in the ribs and called him a "stupid dork," he realized his commanding officer was not being literal. "Yes, Sir…Ma'am, we are on it!"

Cam slowly drove further south about a quarter of a mile. It was a bizarre-looking parade with the ice cream truck in the lead, followed by the worst looking—and sounding—marching band in history. Whistles, air horns, even pots and pans, created a surreal cacophony of unconventional instruments. But it was working, as at first dozens, then hundreds, and then even thousands of herd members paused and tilted their heads at the sound of the music and noise, and then slowly turned and started shuffling toward it.

Of course, some of the more fit zombies did more than shuffle, and within ten minutes the first arrivals reached Becks' troops, but they were quickly and easily dispatched. Becks hoped that before too much of the herd turned, the boats would take over making noise, but when she checked with HQ, she found that most of the vessels were ten to twenty minutes out. Still, they should be able to continue making noise, and when a reasonable amount of zombies had made the turn and started heading in their general direction, they should still have plenty of time to outrun the leading edge and get to safety.

Then everything changed in the blink of an eye.

"You are going to have a lot of company, *real soon*," Henry reported, as the stress in his voice made it crack. "The way you came in, you know, will be full of zombies in a few minutes, so your people should start heading south. Now. *Fast!*"

Apparently the "orange swirls" had been doing their job creating turbulence, as the PDZs were wreaking havoc within the core of the herd. Like a weakened iceberg suddenly giving way, the herd splintered into huge sections. While some still tried to continue to press forward, others tried to go west, and some even did an about-face and started heading south again. By far, however, the bulk of the split herd was now pouring into the woods to the east of the PIP toward a couple of hundred troops and a few snowplows, and a man and a woman in an ice cream truck.

Becks ordered the snowplows to head south in single file and knock down anything or anyone in their path. She told the soldiers to stop making noise, and stay on the non-herd side of the plows and double-quick their asses south beyond the herd, and not to stop for anything until Henry told them it was safe. She was not about to lose anyone in her first real command. And that went for Cam, too. Especially Cam.

"Cam, I want you to get on one of those snowplows and get the hell out of here," Becks ordered, but didn't expect it to be easy.

"Hell, no, Commander. No can do!" Cam said in a manner that Becks had only seen on a couple of other occasions. It was his "concrete wall" demeanor; that rare moment in the life of Cameron Everett, when neither heaven, earth, nor a zombie herd could make him budge. "The ice cream song has to keep playing until the boats take over, or the herd could just start wandering off in some other direction again."

"Yes, but I can drive the truck while you—okay, never mind. I know when I've lost," Becks conceded, as she saw her words were going nowhere.

"Look at it as a win," he replied with that damn, charming smile. "You and me together, turning the tide for humanity, while serving three flavors of soft ice cream and a variety of frozen treats on a stick."

"Just shut up and keep driving," Becks said, unable to suppress a smile.

When the drone footage came into Command HQ, it quickly became evident that at least 75% of the herd had now turned toward the east. A cheer went up, but it was short-lived when they saw that the volunteers between the herd and the cliff were now running for their lives. The mood became even more somber when the ice cream truck was spotted driving back and forth along the access road, continuing to draw the massive herd right toward them.

"Uh, Becks, you might want to consider an evac plan," the general suggested.

"Where are the boats?" Becks simply asked, determined to make this work, one way or another.

"They should be making some noise any second now," he replied, and as if on cue Becks heard the blast of a horn from the river, but it was distant, and faint.

"They will have to do a hell of a lot better than that," Becks stated.

"Here comes the company that Henry was talking about," Cam said, as he stopped the truck and pointed.

It looked like the entire forest itself was moving, and as far as the eye could see from left to right.

"Shit. You're going to have to try to move this truck closer to the river," Becks said as her blood ran cold.

Cam didn't need to be told twice as he spun the wheel and left the access road. They knew they were really painting themselves into a corner—or a cliff as the case may be—but the access road would be overrun before they could make it past the herd. And until they succeeded in getting this mass of zombie corpses to start hurling themselves off the cliff from the force of the undead humanity pushing behind it, there was too much that could go south, literally, as well as north and west. It had to be east, it had to be here, and it had to be now.

"What happens when we get to the edge? Want to have a picnic?" Cam tried to joke with a strained smile as they bounced and rocked through the woods, dodging big stones and fallen tree limbs.

"I'm afraid *we* will be the picnic," Becks replied, making a mental note to save at least two bullets in her revolver. "Let's see what Uncle Sam can do for us."

Becks called HQ to see if their friendly, neighborhood chopper pilots could come and extract them.

"We will be the two idiots on top of the ice cream truck," she added.

They were instructed to try to find a clearing or high point to facilitate their extraction, and their ride was scheduled to arrive in about fifteen minutes.

"It's good to have friends in high places," Cam said with a genuine laugh, clearly relieved that they were not going to either be eaten or drop off the cliff.

Then the ice cream truck slammed to a halt and both Cam and Becks hit the windshield. The force was enough to bloody Cam's nose and split Becks' ear. Both were bleeding profusely, but only momentarily dazed.

"Oh, what fresh hell is this?" Becks asked, gingerly sliding out of her seat onto the ground to assess the situation. "Crap, we're stuck on a pile of rocks. Who the hell puts a pile of rocks in the middle of the woods?"

Becks swore and kicked the side of the truck for good measure. Then she started looking for a sturdy branch to try to make a lever to lift the front end a couple of inches and see if they could back up. What they really needed was Cam's muscle, but he was too injured to be of any help, or worse, be able to run.

Becks now deeply regretted not ordering that Cam should have been forcibly removed from the ice cream truck and carried away, screaming and kicking, if necessary. She dragged a sturdy-looking tree branch over to the front of the truck, jammed it under the axle and used all her strength to try to lift the wheel just enough for Cam to back it off the rocks. The branch immediately snapped, Becks hit the ground, and the back tires spun deeper into the dirt.

"I think we're stuck," Cam announced as Becks rolled her eyes.

"No shit. Let's at least get you on the roof. Like now!" Becks suggested with some urgency, as a large section of the herd was already getting dangerously close.

That was easier said than done, as the numerous wounds in his arms and sides made it impossible for Cam to do the pull-up motion necessary to hoist himself onto the roof. Healthy, he could probably have done it with one hand just to show off, but in his current chewed-up condition there was no way he would make it without help.

They rifled through the contents of the crates and cabinets in the back of the truck, and except for a box of cones that had to be fifty years old which Cam called "dibs" on, there wasn't much that would be of any help. Then Cam found a coil of rope, and Becks instructed him to tie one end around his waist as she scrambled to the roof. Before Cam could tie the rope, however, company had already arrived.

The first unfortunate zombie, a gray-haired man in a torn, pink Izod sweater and golf shoes—and no pants—with festering sores across his thighs and midsection, took simultaneous bullets to the right eye from Cam and one to the left eye from Becks. They exchanged quick glances of approval and Cam motioned that he would take care of the zombies to his right so they didn't duplicate anymore shots and waste ammo. They managed to take down the thirty or so early bird arrivals, which included a bizarre group of women in yoga pants, but the hundreds just behind them, and the tens of thousands behind them would be another story.

The good news was that there were now dozens of boats in the river below making enough noise that Becks suggested it was okay to "shut off the damn music," which felt like an ice pick being removed from her brain

126

when Cam switched it off. The hope that the herd, which now looked as though it was all converging on their position, would fan out a bit was short-lived, as the movement of Becks and Cam was enough for the voracious zombies to hone in on them, and pick up the pace.

Becks hastily tied the rope around her own waist and told Cam to give it all he had. She pulled as hard as she could, and he pulled so hard he tore out half a dozen stitches, but they were still unable to get him onto the roof, and the herd was now within thirty feet.

"HQ, where's our ride?" Becks yelled into the radio. "Things are about to get very crowded here."

"Five minutes out. Sit tight," the pilot himself replied.

"Tell him to step on the gas," Cam said as he took several more shots and then reloaded.

If Becks hadn't been so completely scared out of her mind, she would have been totally fascinated by the scene spreading out before her. She had encountered zombies before, and lots of them, but this was on a scale that was truly mind-boggling. There were people from all walks of life, short and tall, big and small, every nationality and every color imaginable, and even colors that had no business being in human skin, which signaled all manner of infections, diseases, and fungi, and god knows what else.

"Get in the truck until the helicopter arrives," Becks urged, doubting that it would get there before they were surrounded. "And remind me again who came up with the stupid idea of turning the herd?"

Becks flattened herself on the roof of the truck so as not to attract any more attention, but the mass before her was on a beeline straight for them. She was amazed at the terrible sound of moaning, branches breaking, and the incessant pounding of feet in worn shoes, tattered boots, and bare, bloodied, and torn feet. Behind her was the ever-growing din of air horns, bells ringing, music, and shouting. What she didn't hear were the rotors of the helicopter.

Taking a deep breath and then remaining perfectly still, Becks tried to grip the smooth, flat roof as the first wave of zombies crashed into the truck. Cam crouched in the back, hoping not to be seen. The plan was that between Cam, Becks, and the gun crew of the helicopter, they would be able to clear one side of the truck enough to let Cam get out and extract him in the harness, and then just pluck Becks from the roof. If the damn helicopter ever got there, that is.

As another wave of zombies hit the truck with enough force that it started rocking, the beautiful silhouette of the helicopter appeared in the sky to the north. Becks tapped twice on the roof to let Cam know it was near. She tried to remain calm, but the herd continued to pound the truck like waves from an approaching storm—waves filled with deadly sharks, that is. It was awful and terrifying, but as long as the zombies surrounded the truck on all sides it would remain stable. For some reason, however, the zombies quickly gave up on the driver's side of the truck and moved off toward the boat noises, and nearer the cliff.

That left a few hundred zombies pressing against the passenger side, where the front wheel was already up off the ground where they had encountered the pile of rocks. Becks knew it didn't take a physicist to figure out what would happen next.

"Cam, hang on!" she yelled as she slid down across the windshield, just seconds before the ice cream truck heaved over onto its side. Fortunately, the windows remained intact, so Cam should be safe inside, but she was sticking out like a sore thumb—a big, juicy, delicious thumb.

Cam scrambled to the windshield and put his hands against the glass. His expression was one of wild desperation—for her safety—and he started yelling for her to run. Thrusting her left hand forward, she put it against his on the other side of the glass, their eyes locked for a second, and then she turned and took off like a bat out of hell.

Captain Lennox and his men were stunned as they witnessed most of the massive herd suddenly turn and head east. Very few of the PDZs followed as there were still plenty of regular zombies left to kill, and their orange heads now stood out prominently amongst the others that remained on the Palisades Interstate Parkway. The numbers of zombies on the roadway was still staggering and overwhelming, but he now saw hope in the "divide and conquer" strategy of attacking the separated sections with all the PDZs and troops they could gather. First, of course, a few hundred thousand zombies needed to take a long walk off a short cliff.

Lennox asked HQ whether they should resume the attack, and whether they should stay on the Western Front or go after the northern or southern sections of the herd that had broken away. There was some serious discussion at HQ, and drone footage was reviewed, and re-reviewed, but the ultimate decision was to "wait and see." The last thing they wanted to have was the sound of gunfire drawing the groups back together.

Phil had snuck into command headquarters and was harassing a private for information on Becks, Cam, and all of the volunteers, many of whom he knew. The private had no idea who this man in the lab coat was, or why he was in the command center, but as Phil was clearly someone important—and the private wanted to get this doctor off his back as soon as possible—he gave him a quick rundown on the situation.

The snowplows had made their way back onto the PIP and led the troops to relative safety behind the herd, but tens of thousands of zombies were still headed their way.

Captain Lennox, the Army, and the militia were well-entrenched on the Western Front, with a sizable wall of zombie corpses piled up along an almost half-mile line. The PDZs were helping by continuing to attack the zombies along the other side of that line of the section of the herd which now appeared as if it was getting boxed in.

The northbound section of the herd was technically still moving forward, but almost imperceptibly. The two divisions had inflicted enough casualties along the leading edge that it was a tangled mass of limbs and guts, with thousands of zombies swarming over the remains to feed. The entire mass was being pushed forward due to the sheer weight behind it, but the resistance was causing more and more zombies to look for a path of easier movement, which would hopefully lead even more to the east, and eventually, the cliff.

Which brought the private to that great, eastern exodus. He was almost bubbly with joy explaining how this enormous herd of zombies was heading "to their doom," a phrase he used with glee several times. The drone footage made it appear as if the entire landscape itself was sliding inexorably toward the rocky cliff. It was an awe-inspiring sight, but Phil was not exactly bubbly when the private told him that it looked like Cam was trapped in an overturned ice cream truck and Becks was on the run.

"Well, what the hell are you doing about it?" Phil shouted, wanting so much to smack the grin off the private's face, and apparently looking as if he was about to do it.

The private actually put up a hand in a defensive motion, and then slowly lowered it after a few seconds.

"They sent a helicopter," he offered, now looking quite serious as his bubbles were burst. "They're doing what they can, but there's no way to get that guy out of the truck with the herd swarming all over it, and the lady took off and we don't currently know her exact position."

Much to the private's dismay, Phil pulled up a chair right next to him and announced that he would not move until his friends were safe.

Becks ran for her life, but she didn't know where she was going; she was just going as fast as she could through the woods to put as much distance as possible between herself and the herd. She didn't get very far, however, before she tripped on the rope still tied around her waist and did a head-first dive into a thorn bush. As much as it hurt falling into the profusely barbed branches, it hurt twice as much pulling herself out of it. Once free, she just gathered up the loose section of rope, rather than trying to untie it, as she thought she might need it if she had to climb a tree to escape the herd. Of course, she was planning on it not coming to that.

The helicopter was now over the area, but the dense tree cover was too thick to signal her location. Her best bet was to go toward the cliff where she would be able to tell the pilot to look for her. Behind her, the herd seemed to stretch out as far as she could see in both directions and it was moving in fast, especially from the south. That section must have broken away first and was moving north and east at an alarming pace.

Becks burst out of the tree line and skidded to a stop just a few feet from the edge of the cliff. Not usually one to be afraid of heights, her current high anxiety level made her head spin as she glanced at the treacherous drop before her. Forcing herself to look up, all of the dozens of boats in the river were a welcome sight, and she wished more than anything to be on one of them right now.

"This is Commander Truesdale, I am at the edge of the cliff awaiting extraction," she said into her radio. "Any word on Cam back in the ice cream truck?"

"Coming your way ASAP," the pilot responded. "I'll pick you up and then we'll see what we can do about Cam, but it looks like Times Square on New Year's Eve down there, and the party is headed your way."

Becks felt very guilty about leaving Cam all alone in the midst of a few hundred thousand zombies, but if he stayed still and quiet, they should just pass by him. Even if she had her Humvee and .50 cal there wouldn't be anything she could do on the ground anyway. There may not even be anything they could do from the air, but it was worth a try. Becks didn't want to attempt to radio Cam and make any kind of noise, so she would just have to be patient and hope that he would contact headquarters.

Phil grabbed the shoulder of the private when he heard that Becks was just moments away from being rescued and shook the poor soldier two or three times. Phil was going to have to have a little chat with Becks when she returned to West Point and let her know that *his* nerves couldn't stand *her* dangerous situations any longer.

"You are a sight for sore eyes," Becks said, waving to the pilot who had swung around over the river and was now facing the cliff.

"We have a visual. Moving in," the pilot announced, and then added, "Step back as far as possible, it's about to get windy down there."

Becks got as close as she could to the tree line, but couldn't go too far or the harness would get tangled in the branches. The cliff cut in several feet deeper on either side of her, and about a dozen zombies—led by a dark-haired woman in her underwear, which after a year or more of death and no hygiene was not a pretty sight—were no more than forty feet from her position. A harness was being lowered out of the side door of the helicopter as it made its approach, and Becks shifted her weight toward the tree line and her back foot as she raised her right arm in preparation to grab her lifeline to safety.

"A little more, a little more ..." Becks said as the downdraft from the rotors was making the harness swing, and making it more difficult for her to maintain her precarious balance.

The harness swung overhead just beyond her fingertips, but on the backswing it looked like it had been lowered, so she stepped forward to grab it. Just as her hand made contact with the straps, the dirt at the edge of the cliff gave way, due to all the recent rain. The next few seconds were like one of those recurring nightmares where she felt herself falling and struggled to grab something, but could only find thin air.

The brief nightmare seemed to end, however, as her foot slid down about eight or ten inches, but then caught something solid. Becks froze, afraid to move even an inch further until she was sure the ground was stable. The helicopter backed away so as not to blow her off the cliff.

"You okay down there?" the concerned pilot asked.

"Yeah, I think so," Becks whispered, as if the sound of her own voice might cause too much vibration. "Well, that certainly scared the shit out of—ahhhh!"

Just as she started to back away from the edge, a foot-wide section crumbled away in a cascade of pebbles and mud. Becks screamed as she threw herself face down and clawed at the ground trying to find anything to grasp onto. Nothing but smooth bedrock met her fingernails as she slid slowly, but inevitably, toward the edge. As her body dangled from the waist down, her legs flailed back and forth, looking for a toehold. Time almost stood still, except for the measured grinding of her nails across the rock in little pulses that seemed to match her wildly beating heart.

"To your left! To your left!" the pilot was shouting as he watched helplessly from a distance. If he dared move any closer the downdraft could be fatal.

Becks held her breath and shot a quick glance down to her left and saw that a column of rock was only a couple of feet away. If she reached for it with her hand and missed, that would be the end, so she lifted her left foot and mercifully was able to get her leg on the top of the column, which was roughly the size and shape of a foot rest on a recliner, with the long side jutting out from the cliff. The entire column had broken away hundreds of years ago from the repeated action of freezing and thawing, but it had only fallen a short distance where it had wedged itself into a split in an outcropping the size of an upright bathtub. None of this meant a damn thing to Becks at the moment, as all she cared about was that she had stopped her fall, for now.

It was like a torturous and deadly game of Twister, and a false move would likely be her last move. Pulling as hard as she could with her outstretched left leg, she managed to inch herself over enough to hook her ankle over the far edge of the column. With the extra leverage, she shifted over just enough that the moment she completely lost her grip on the edge, she plopped down hard, straddling the top of the column. Not that she was complaining about the rough landing, as the alternative landing would have been infinitely rougher.

There wasn't much chance that she would be able to stand on the top of the column and pull herself back onto the slick and slippery cliff, but she didn't have to. Wrapping the end of the rope through a crack in the rock, and around a few more times for good measure, she was in a secure enough position for the helicopter to move back in.

"Can we try this again?" Becks asked the pilot, waving one of her hands, bloodied from the desperate clawing on the bedrock.

"I will if you stop trying to give me a heart attack," the pilot replied, greatly relieved that he didn't have to witness a gruesome tragedy. "But we have to move fast as your company is almost to the edge."

The helicopter moved forward and that beautiful harness was now just a few feet above her when something slammed into Becks upturned face and almost made her black out. Dazed and completely confused, she shook her head and tried to focus her eyes and saw a filthy, bare foot right in front of her.

"What the fuck!" she shouted, still not comprehending what had happened.

Just as the harness was being lowered, the underwear-clad female zombie had slipped over the cliff right above her head, and her leg had gone straight into the harness and she had kicked Becks squarely in the jaw. The foul-smelling zombie was now tangled in the harness and spinning rapidly, her arms and legs threatening to slam into Becks with every revolution, causing her to lean face down as far as possible. Even still, Becks received a few more punches and kicks which almost pushed her over.

"Back off, back off!" Becks yelled, as the pilot pulled over the river to get the rotating zombie away from her.

No sooner was Underwear Girl clear, however, when a much larger man in what actually appeared to be some sort of a sequined, circus performer costume fell over the edge, landing chest-first onto Becks' column of rock and grabbing onto her leg. Fortunately, she was able to ram her boot into his mouth before getting bitten, but the strength of his bite felt as though he was crushing her toes.

The more immediate concern, however, was that his large girth and thrashing motion would push her off the column. Becks drew her revolver and aimed it at the man's head, but he was like a crazed predator shaking its prey—her foot—and she was afraid she would shoot herself in the process. Instead, she pressed the barrel down onto the vertebra that was right above the man's heart and squeezed the trigger.

Circus Man immediately ceased to struggle as his heart was ripped to pieces by the large caliber bullet. Blood poured out of him and Becks found herself sitting in a stinking, ZIPs-infested pool of it, but she had no time to dwell on how disgusting it was or how uncomfortable it felt. She had to push his body off the column, which was quite a struggle and almost caused her to fall a few times.

As Circus Man was finally bouncing along the cliff face on his way to the bottom, however, the pilot yelled, "Incoming! You need to move. Now!"

"*Move where!?*" Becks yelled back, throwing up her hands.

"Base of the column on the right. There's a crevice I think you can squeeze into."

It didn't sound like the greatest vote of confidence, but it wasn't like she had any other options. Another two zombies plummeted over the edge, just to her right and left, but according to the pilot this trickle was about to become an avalanche as the main herd was rapidly closing in on her position.

Becks looked down and saw what the pilot was talking about, but she would have to use the rope to lower herself down, and if she didn't fit into this crevice, there would be no coming back. However, when a young girl in pigtails literally fell into her lap and tried to bite her, she knew it was now or never.

Flinging the girl aside like a rag doll, Becks tugged hard on the rope to make sure it would hold her weight. Taking a deep breath, she took a "leap of faith" and swung her left leg over the column. Dropping several feet with a gasp, the rope finally caught and held. The crevice was about the width of the space beneath a bed, but less than two feet deep. It was filled with feathery little roots, smelly fungus, trickling water, and dense spider webs, but as Becks wedged herself into it, it felt as comforting as a king-sized bed in a luxury hotel. The instant her head and body cleared the surface of the cliff face, three more adult zombies fell right in front of her. Before Becks could tell the pilot she was okay, it was like the floodgates suddenly opened and a steady stream of zombies started dropping over the cliff.

Some hit the column of rock before bouncing off, and some hung onto the column for a moment before several of his or her companions knocked him off, and others fell straight down—headfirst, feet first, or spiraling. A few that fell feet first and facing the cliff looked at Becks as they passed with blank stares, having no clue that they were about two seconds away from being splattered on the boulders below.

It was very cramped quarters standing wedged into the crevice in the rock, but Becks was able to reach her radio and let the pilot know that she was safe, and never before in her life did she appreciate how relative a term could be in its meaning. The pilot responded that there was nothing he could do right now, but he would land at the Exit 5 depot and be on call for the moment he could help.

Becks thought back to that magical weekend she and Cam had spent at Niagara Falls soon after they had met, where she was to realize for the first time in her life that she was in love. When they actually left their hotel room, they did some sightseeing and had donned those silly plastic ponchos and gone into a tunnel that opened behind the falls. The sound and power of the water crashing down in front of them was something Becks would never forget, and she thought she would never experience anything like it again.

Now Niagara was eclipsed by the cascade of zombies pouring over the cliff in an ever-widening line of self–destruction. This sound of countless bodies hurtling down to be smashed and broken on the rocks below was indescribable and nauseating, and Becks tried to be clinical about it to deal with the horror.

"Skull. Skull. Tibia. Rib cage," she said out loud as if playing some grotesque form of Bingo, trying to guess which bones were shattering by their sound. But the attempt at a distraction didn't last long, as soon so many bodies were falling at once that all of the snapping, crunching, and cracking melded together in what sounded like the world's largest demolition derby with nonstop high-speed collisions between hundreds and hundreds of cars.

After a while she just shut her eyes to it all and put her hands over her ears. This was the outcome she had planned and prayed for—the bulk of the herd heading towards the cliff and being pushed over the edge, doing to themselves what the Army, volunteers, and PDZs couldn't hope to do during weeks of battle. But now that she was witnessing their demise up close and personal, and she could see their faces and hear their bones splintering, Becks couldn't help but think back to the people that they were—the parents, spouses, co-workers, friends, lovers, and enemies that lived in all of the houses, drove all of those cars, and ate in all the restaurants that now were dark and empty.

Becks was trapped in a scene out of hell that even Dante couldn't imagine, and after a couple of hours, she feared it might drive her mad. Then over the din of the pounding bodies and blasting boat horns, her radio crackled with a burst of static. After another crackle of static, a voice broke in.

"Commander Truesdale, this is Combat Headquarters. Are you okay?" someone asked awkwardly, realizing the stupidity of such a question to a woman wedged into a cliff covered in falling zombies— something *everyone* in West Point was watching, thanks to Henry's drone feed.

"Just peachy, thanks for asking," Becks replied, glad to hear another living being.

"Wanted to let you know that Cam just contacted us. He's still surrounded, but safe inside the truck. We did inform him of your situation, and he wanted us to...well...to play a song for you," the soldier said, sounding even more awkward. "It took a while to find it, but we have it if you want to hear it."

It must be a love song or something inspirational, or maybe the song they played at our wedding for our first dance, Becks thought, and told the soldier to proceed.

There were several seconds of silence, two more bursts of static, and then some music and lyrics she couldn't place started blasting. It was some sort of 1980s dance music, which wasn't something either of them *ever* listened to, but it soon became clear as the singing female duo belted out the refrain to the ridiculous song.

"It's raining men! Hallelujah, it's raining men!"

The tremendous stress, tension, and fear of her predicament suddenly vanished, at least for a few minutes, and Becks began laughing so hard that if she wasn't so tightly packed into a rock crevice she would have fallen to her knees.

By the time that the silly hit song by the Weather Girls had finished, Becks had tears streaming down her cheeks and her lungs actually hurt from the unrestrained laughter. When she was finally able to talk, she asked headquarters to relay a message to Cam, who had once again known exactly what to do to give her the renewed strength and resolve to go on.

"Tell Cam he's an asshole…and that's why I love him."

As darkness fell, the base of the cliff was deep with bodies stretching along hundreds of yards of shoreline. Most of the smashed zombies rolled off into the water so that a steady line of battered corpses was now floating down the river toward the George Washington Bridge—back where they came from—looking very much like thousands of pieces of twisted driftwood.

The people in the boats continued making a racket, and had even started a second group farther south, hoping to entice the section of the herd that had done an about-face to head toward the river. The Snowplow Division, as HQ was calling them, had finally stopped their retreat and had used the trucks, and anything else they could find, to block the PIP and "encourage" that part of the herd to the east to another section of cliff that would also be an excellent location for zombies to push one another to their final death.

Along the way, the troops had come upon the home of Joanna Gilchrist, who came out of her house and gasped in wonder at so many living, breathing humans. She had thought for a very long time that she was the last person on earth. She also felt more dead than the zombies that threatened her. At the sight of so many people—more than she had seen since the start of quarantine—Joanna fell to her knees and sobbed until she passed out. One of the female soldiers, who had twisted an ankle, volunteered to stay with the woman in her house, and her friends promised to return for them soon—which was another of those very relative terms in the midst of a zombie apocalypse.

On the Western Front, Captain Lennox and his troops were catching some rest. The melee between the western section of the herd and the PDZs continued unabated. It seemed as though a PDZ would rather kill than eat, which was an unexpected benefit. The number of mounds of bodies, and those zombies eating them, kept growing at an impressive rate. HQ had asked if they should be creating more PDZs, but Lennox advised them to hold off and see what the morning's light revealed. After all, even if the herd was totally eliminated, there would still be a lot of PDZs to deal with, as well, and they were the biggest and strongest of them all.

The best news was from Margo and Sticky Pete's divisions on the northern perimeter. As it became harder and harder for the zombies trying to push forward, because of all the bodies on the ground, they started filtering to the east, along the same paths as their companions who were currently falling over the cliff. It started with just a handful, but as had often been seen with the "herd mentality" of the ZIPs, the majority of them suddenly, and simultaneously, turned as a unit.

While it was still light, Command HQ had estimated the northern section to be between 70,000 and 80,000 strong, and everyone was very impressed that they were able to come up with this number. What no one realized was that they arrived at this calculation by recalling the crowd size at the Army Black Knights football home games at Michie Stadium at West Point, which had a capacity of 38,000. Using Henry's drone imagery, the general staff figured the northern section to contain about twice that number of people.

It was wonderful news that this huge threat to the Hudson Valley might continue to destroy itself. There were two people, however, who weren't completely thrilled. Cam was still stuck in the overturned ice cream truck. Now that it was dark, even if there was a break or opening it wouldn't be safe, given that he wouldn't be able to see or run. And now that the capacity of two Army-Navy games was also headed his way, he would just have to lay low and whisper occasional messages to HQ to be relayed to Becks. As bad as he had it, though, he had five-star accommodations compared to the hell she was enduring.

"I just want to get off my feet for a few minutes!" Becks shouted in pain and frustration.

Every muscle burned and ached, and her legs were cramping after so many hours of standing wedged into the crevice. She wasn't even able to stretch her arm or leg outside of her craggy nook as any one of the countless falling bodies could cause her serious injury. She had managed to reach for her canteen and an energy bar, but the past ordeals in New York City and Albany, not to mention the long hours in the lab, had taken their toll and she just wanted to sleep.

At times of great stress and discomfort—which Becks had decided had happened way too often in recent years—her mind often did not settle on thoughts that helped her situation. As an example, for a solid twenty minutes she recalled every detail of the paper she had once read on the physiological and psychological effects of "Positional Torture," basically where prisoners were forced to remain standing for days at a time. Pain became excruciating, delirium and hallucinations were common, and ultimately, if taken to its cruel and inevitable conclusion, the victim would succumb to circulatory failure.

Realizing she was not thinking the most productive thoughts, she requested that HQ keep contacting her and try to keep her mind occupied. Around midnight, a steady stream of well-wishes began being patched through to her from friends and coworkers from West Point, Cam's compound, Fort Ace, and troops in the field. They really helped her to focus and fight through the pain—and growing feeling of claustrophobia. The drainpipe in which she had spent that winter night was spacious by comparison, although she was glad to have spiders this time instead of rats.

The best medicine was from Phil, who had been sleeping on and off in that same chair in HQ. The private he initially bothered was off duty, but the replacement was still feeding him updates. When he heard that Becks needed distractions, he ran back to the lab and returned with a stack of status updates and problems that needed solving.

Science was both Rebecca Truesdale's refuge and purpose in life. Challenged by equations, puzzled by anomalous data, and fixated on stats and results, she was transported from her tiny, rock prison to a place where her brain was free and her pain was forgotten. Phil was always impressed with Becks' mind, but to hear it perform so flawlessly under such horrendous conditions was a privilege to behold.

Dawn over the Hudson River was a beautiful sight—what Becks could see of it through falling corpses. A short time before sunrise, there had been a brief, blessed, period where no bodies fell past her. Theoretically, she could have been extracted during that time—if the helicopter was already in the air, and if they knew for sure how long the zombie-free window would be. Unfortunately, Becks had waited a couple of minutes before calling HQ to make sure it was a real break, and then by the time the helicopter pilot was lifting off from the Exit 5 depot the "Hudson River Falls" had resumed its gruesome cascade of bodies over the cliff. At least Becks had taken the opportunity to stretch her stiff arms and legs.

She had even taken a great risk and held on tightly to the rope so she could tilt her body backwards out of the crevice for a minute. The resulting rush of blood to her head made everything spin and her ears pound, but it felt *so* good to upend herself for even a short time.

She would have loved to remain upside down for a little bit longer, but the crack of branches and the shuffle of feet overhead signaled that another wave of lemming zombies was headed her way. There was a moment of panic when she went to pull herself upright and her arms felt like jello, but adrenaline pumped her into overdrive and she was safely wedged back into her crevice before the leading edge of this latest section was being pushed off the cliff.

Henry and his drone team were back in action with the first light, and Becks was thrilled to hear that the ice cream truck might be in the clear within two or three hours. More good news came when Henry reported that the southern section of the herd had reached the edge of the palisades a couple of miles to the south and, with the unstoppable force of tens of thousands of zombies drawn by the sounds in the river, had just begun pushing one another over the cliff.

Small splinter groups of several hundreds, or even a thousand or so zombies, had wandered off into New Jersey, which could seriously inhibit efforts there, but Project Decimation had been battle tested and proven effective, and the rules of engagement from here on out would be rewritten. Perhaps it was the beginning of the end of the apocalypse in the Hudson Valley and surrounding regions?

Chapter 18

Command HQ didn't know that so many people were still alive in the Northeast, and in good fighting shape, as individuals and small communities scattered from Pennsylvania to Maine were converging on West Point by the thousands. There were even a lot of people coming down from Canada, with one group saying they would rather face a zombie megaherd than another brutal Canadian winter.

One couldn't help wondering if this cohesion and determination had been exhibited *after* quarantine, that maybe the worst of the apocalypse could have been averted. Of course, hindsight is always 20/20, and your average accountant, student, sales clerk, and factory worker didn't know squat back then about survival and fighting. It only took a matter of weeks for civilization to completely collapse, but years for people to be forged in the fire of desperation and learn how to rise up and take back what they had lost.

Deciding to strike while the iron was hot and when adequate personnel was available, these waves of volunteers were immediately sent out to the Exit 5 depot to be deployed into the field wherever they were most needed. Many of them were shocked to see all of the orange-haired PDZs attacking their fellow zombies, but it gave everyone hope that the human race was no longer fighting a losing battle—or fighting alone.

There was an unfortunate incident where a young teen from Vermont—who may have consumed way too much liquid courage—didn't fully comprehend the nature of the PDZs and thought he could put one on a leash and use it like an attack dog. The boy's screams quickly became unintelligible gurgling, and then there was silence, as his "pet PDZ" tore into his throat and was quickly joined by several other regular zombies who were getting their first taste of fresh meat in ages.

At the start of infection, the sight of a young boy being eviscerated would have been completely demoralizing and sent the general population running to hide. But anyone left standing at this point had witnessed and experienced so many horrors that "one drunken idiot's death" wasn't going to stop them.

Captain Lennox quickly welcomed and integrated these fresh troops into his forces and knew right where to send them for maximum effect.

Margo and Sticky Pete kind of looked at each other with a "now what are we supposed to do?" expression, as they had suddenly become senior field commanders, but they somehow managed to wing it. Reinforcements had no way to reach the Snowplow Division, but their small numbers were holding their own and just letting zombie nature take its course as the herd marched onward to the cliff.

As the sun rose, the temperature did, as well, and by midmorning it was already an unusually hot day. That heat made Becks extra sleepy and she fought to keep her eyes open. Twice, she nodded off for a few seconds, but managed to catch herself before falling out of the crevice. Her shoulder did take a glancing blow from a falling body when she leaned too far out the third time she fell asleep, and that snapped her back to full wakefulness for a while, but the struggle with fatigue, dehydration, and pain was quickly wearing her down.

"Don't know…how much longer…I can take this," she radioed to HQ as she fought the impulse to just give up.

"Oh, don't be such a crybaby," came the response from an all-too familiar voice.

"Cam, you're safe!?" Becks yelled, feeling life returning to her numbed limbs.

"Cameron Everett has left the ice cream truck!" he announced, and then explained how Sticky Pete had taken an impressive force of 2,000 volunteers and cleared a path through the remnants of the trailing edge of the herd to reach his position. They were stretchering him back to the road where—against his wishes—they would be taking him to West Point.

"Uh…I wish I could say they were on their way to get you," he said with some hesitation, "but the herd is still pretty thick."

"Tell them not to risk all those people just for me. I used to pull all-nighters in the ER, filled with gangbangers and crazy people, so I guess I can manage watching a zombie waterfall for a little bit longer."

Several more hours of torture ensued as Becks did everything she could to battle the extreme heat, her cramping muscles, and sheer exhaustion, but even Phil's equations stopped helping as her mind began to wander. The instant she was unable to calculate the square root of 173, Phil informed the commanding general that they had to do something ASAP!

The helicopter and its gun crew were immediately notified and within minutes were airborne and headed for Becks' position. Thousands of zombies were still pressing one another toward and over the cliff, but with Becks fading they had to try to clear the section right above her. Getting as close to the cliff as he dared, the pilot turned the craft sideways so one of the gun crews could lay down a clear and almost level field of fire. Becks covered her ears as the impressive, large caliber automatic weapon carved a bloody path of destruction twenty feet wide and at least thirty feet deep. Even with all of the mutilated bodies and body parts that the other zombies now fell upon to consume, it wouldn't be long before the thousands behind them surged forward, so they had to act fast.

Once again, the pilot got into position, and lowered the harness, only this time a former member of search and rescue was in that harness. When he reached Becks and found her semi-delirious, he didn't hesitate to smack her in the face and shouted at her to focus. With wildly shaking hands, she was able to help him attach another harness around her torso and legs. Then she found the strength to use her combat knife to cut the rope that had saved her life.

"Get me the fuck out of here, please," she whispered, and then collapsed into his arms while the helicopter veered up and away.

Phil practically knocked the original private—now back on duty—right out of his seat with a vigorous slap on the back when the pilot radioed HQ that Becks was safely on board. He then ran over to the hospital to inform Cam, but word had already spread and celebrations were taking place everywhere at West Point. It seems that despite all that was going on, *everyone* was anxiously following every minute of the ordeal of Dr. Rebecca Truesdale.

Chapter 19

Across the hallowed grounds of West Point are statues and monuments representing people and events that have shaped American history. For example, George Washington astride his horse, Sylvanus Thayer, the "Father of the Military Academy," and the stately column of the Battlefield Monument at Trophy Point dedicated to the brave soldiers of the Civil War. Then there are the statues of World War II legends— MacArthur, Eisenhower, and Patton.

Arguably, however, none of these symbols of our country's freedom, and the people who fought and died for it, will draw the attention of cadets and visitors in the coming generations more than the newest monument, lovingly placed atop a platform of stones carried by the hands of hundreds of Army regulars, volunteer soldiers, and ordinary citizens. This tribute to the "Battle of the Palisades" is unlike any other, and indeed, given the nature of the enemy, it should be different than anything throughout the millennia of military history.

In a place of honor at the edge of the parade ground, perched on its crude base of rocks, now rests the famous ice cream truck. After the battle, people banded together to upright the truck and tow it out of the woods and back onto the PIP, where the grandson of the man who landed on the beaches of Normandy on D-Day, proudly drove it to West Point.

Along the route, cheering people lined the roadways as the battered vehicle rumbled along. Its iconic ice cream music, which had proven to be capable of drawing to it both the living and the dead, echoed through the Hudson Valley as the procession was broadcast via radio by the Voice of the Hudson as part of the celebration of the victory in the Battle of the Palisades, preserving the fragile renaissance of civilization throughout the region.

Hundreds of thousands of zombies from the New York City herd had plunged over the cliffs along the Hudson River. What used to be one of the most scenic vistas in the country was now a junkyard of corpses piled in towering heaps stretching for miles. While the countless bodies that had tumbled into the river would soon pass out to sea and disappear beneath the waves, the mountains of flesh along the riverbanks were another story. These rotting masses may be there for years, perhaps even decades. But the zombies were now dead and gone forever, and no longer a threat—unlike the tens of thousands of fellow herd members that still tried to spread out through northern New Jersey and southern New York.

Once the last of the eastern and southern sections of the herd had gone over the cliff, their companions had to be dealt with before they could wander too far. A thousand new PDZs were created to be the first wave of what had been transformed from a desperate defense to a carefully planned offense. Experience now taught everyone how best to use the Project Decimation zombie soldiers, which was primarily to disrupt consolidated herd movements, and distract and splinter large groups into ever smaller, more manageable sections.

Not that there was anything manageable about 500 or 1,000 ravenous undead corpses headed straight for you, but at least with the many thousands of volunteers who had come from far and wide, they now had the firepower to slowly, but constantly, chip away at the zombies. Still, it was very dangerous business, as too many people were to discover.

A militia group of seventeen men and women from Ontario had followed about a hundred zombies down a dead end street lined with chain link fences. The Canadian fighters thought they would box in the zombies and pick them off in a matter of minutes. What they didn't know was that over 300 zombies had followed the Canadians to that location and *they* were the ones who became boxed in. Their terrified cries for help over the radio slowly dwindled to a lone voice whispering, "It's too late…"

Some boys from Red Hook, New York, who had come of age during the apocalypse, had done more than their fair share of hunting and killing zombies, and thought they were capable of handling anything, so they decided to go off on their own. They started pursuing some stragglers through the woods and after a while it seemed almost like a video game, as they were all excellent shots and in superior physical condition.

None of that mattered, however, when they found themselves near the edge of the cliff with more than a thousand "stragglers" all headed their way. Only one of the boys somehow managed to fight his way back to the main body of troops. Although severely bitten, he would survive, but he would never be able to erase the memory of witnessing the blood and screams of his friends being slaughtered and consumed.

Too many of these fatal incidents occurred until Captain Lennox took overall command of all the soldiers in the field—volunteers and regulars—and set down the rules of engagement. Essentially, if you wanted to stay alive, you followed orders and didn't go rogue. Under Lennox's command, there were less casualties in two weeks than there had been in those chaotic first few days.

At the end of those two weeks, victory was declared and the biohazard teams began the unenviable task of clearing the bodies. There was no way they could bury all of those corpses, which in many cases were just dismembered limbs and piles of guts. Cremation would have consumed way too much precious firewood, on which the majority of people in the Hudson Valley still relied for cooking and heat.

As the riverbanks beneath the cliff were already like the depths of hell, it was decided to scoop up all of the remains and dump them over the edge, as well. All of these rotting, contaminated body parts would create a major ZIPs' breeding ground in the Hudson River, but West Point scientists had already begun new projects to kill ZIPs' eggs and larvae in the river, and sterilize mature parasites.

Phil's obvious choice to head these projects was Dr. Rebecca Truesdale, as she was one of the leading authorities on the ZIPs, and it was the only way to keep her from going back out in the field to fight. When they had brought Becks back to West Point she was in pretty rough shape, but three days of nothing but sleeping and eating brought back her strength—although it would take another week or so for all of the swollen spider bites to subside.

Cam had been in much better shape, and after he was re-stitched and had a good night's sleep he was doing well—but still in no shape to go back down to the fight. After a few days of grumbling, he was officially appointed as the "Commander of Survivor Tactics and Methods," a new post created to teach everyone—from the general staff to the kitchen staff—how to find food, make shelter, and most importantly, fight.

This latest crisis clearly illustrated how unprepared so many people were, even after all that had happened. It was obvious that many people had survived just by tagging along with more capable companions, while others survived simply by sheer dumb luck. Even those who had fought and scavenged their way out of quarantine discovered that they were not prepared to face something like the New York City herd. Cam's job was to bring every man, woman, and child in the area up to a level of training and preparedness to deal with *whatever* the future of the apocalypse may throw at them.

The Columbia students now headed the Project Decimation teams and were already hard at work designing and implanting "kill switches" in PDZs, which actually were not just meant to neutralize a zombie soldier. The function of these electrodes implanted in the back of the skull was to stun the PDZ by remote control to prepare him for transport without the need of getting close to it. If a PDZ was threatening people, or had outlived its usefulness, a greater charge was applied, frying its ZIPs' brain network.

It didn't take long before they had Jaws fitted with a prototype and had been field testing him in New Jersey. The troops down there all wanted to know when they were going to get their own squads of Jaws. The main holdup to wide scale deployment was trying to find a sufficient power source. They had literally bolted a small solar panel to Jaws' head to keep his kill switch powered, but that clearly wasn't practical in the long run. The team was supremely confident they would figure out something, as they had both experience and the optimism of youth on their side.

Other changes also appeared destined for the area. After World War II, many of the soldiers who had passed through Camp Shanks on their way to battlefields across the world, decided to return to the Hudson Valley to live and raise their families. Likewise, many of the volunteers who had left their isolated communities for hundreds of miles around found it very appealing to have farms, and real towns—with running water and electricity!—not to mention a functioning military base. And other than the festering piles of zombie corpses along the palisades, it was a beautiful area.

More than any of that, though, was the feeling of being part of something again. Humanity had lost more than their homes, businesses, and lives—they had lost their humanity, and what it meant to be part of the human family. A few former realtors from Rockland and Orange Counties volunteered to start a housing program, matching new arrivals with suitable, and safe, homes and property, of which there was an abundant supply.

This would all mean that more schools would be needed, and more medical facilities, farmland, factories, etc.—basically more of everything, but these were good problems to have—very good in lieu of the fact that just a short time ago a massive herd of death and destruction was threatening to obliterate everything in its path and turn the Hudson Valley into a merciless and hopeless killing field.

Chapter 20

One warm, sunny day, Becks actually sat by the river with a cup of tea and a book. Of course, the book was on parasitology, but it was still out of character for her to work outside the lab. Although she was much better, every morning she still asked Cam to get her clothes out of the closet, as she couldn't even stand that much of a confined space. The crevice and falling zombie nightmares were as vivid and terrifying now as they were a few weeks earlier, but with all she had suffered, Becks never expected to sleep well ever again.

Any normal person would not have been able to endure all of the physical torture and mental anguish she had been through since the start of infection, and indeed, there were special rest homes springing up for survivors who had simply lost their minds. But nothing was normal about Becks, and while she hoped to never again encounter the many horrors she had suffered, she knew in the core of her being that she would be ready to face any challenge with both her brains and strength.

As her mind wandered across the wrecked landscape of her life since her days as a nurse, a researcher, and a student, her focus suddenly centered on a solitary object floating down the river. It could have been just a piece of driftwood, or it could have been the corpse of the zombie or a person.

As she closed her book and headed back to the lab she thought, *All I know is it's not me, and I'm going to continue to do everything in my power to keep it that way.*

The End

The first novel in the series, *HVZA: Hudson Valley Zombie Apocalypse*, is available in paperback and e-books.

"...heart pumping, page turning action..."

"...gripping, on the edge of your seat read from beginning to end..."

"This book has just the right mix of science, horror, action, tragedy, humor, and (ultimately) hope."

ISBN: 978-1-937174-15-6

The second novel in the series, *HVZA 2: Hudson Valley Zombie Apocalypse*, is available in paperback and e-books.

"Bloody good."

"An honest boots on the ground experience set in the middle of a zombie apocalypse. Follow the further adventures of Dr. Rebecca Truesdale, aka, "Becks," as she once again finds herself surrounded by hordes of the hungry dead in Hell on Earth, aka New Jersey!"

ISBN: 978-1-937174-24-8

The graphic companion to the first *HVZA* novel,
eight different teams of artists explore the characters and events
of the zombie apocalypse.

"A truly imaginative Zombie Anthology. Full of stories for every appetite."
-- Paul J. Salamoff, Writer/Producer (Discord, Logan's Run: Last Day)

"One of the coolest collections of independent comic book writers and
artists take on the world of horror with this collection of unique tales!"
-- Darren Davis, publisher of Bluewater Comics

"Not since peanut butter and chocolate has there been as perfect a
combination as zombies and comics! What's better than one zombie story?
How about a whole brain-eating collection of zombie stories?!"
--Jim Salicrup, Editor-in-Chief, Papercutz and former Marvel Comics editor
on "The Avengers," "The Amazing Spider-Man," "The Uncanny X-Men"
and "The Fantastic Four."

ISBN 978-1937174-18-7

About the Author

Linda Zimmermann is no stranger to the undead. She is the author of the popular *Ghost Investigator* series of books which chronicle her actual ghost hunting adventures. In addition, she is the award-winning author of science and history books.

She enjoys lecturing on a wide variety of topics, and has spoken at the Smithsonian Institution, Gettysburg, West Point, and several national Mensa events. Linda has also made numerous appearances on radio and television, and at science fiction and comic book conventions. Her first UFO book, *In the Night Sky*, was made into an award-winning documentary in which she was featured.

When she isn't glued to her computer writing books, Linda goes cycling, kayaking, cross country skiing, and snowshoeing. She is a lifelong NY Mets and NY Giants fan, so don't even think of trying to call her when a game is on.

As a vegetarian, if Linda ever turned into a zombie, she would have to subsist on brain-flavored tofu.

www.gotozim.com

www.hvzombie.com

www.ghostinvestigator.com

https://www.facebook.com/hudsonvalleyufos

http://www.badsciences.com/bad-science

Linda Zimmermann's books are available from her websites, Amazon, Barnes & Noble, and most major retailers. They are also available for Kindle, Apple, NookBook, Kobo, and other E-book formats.

Which do you prefer?
Vote for your favorite at:

http://www.hvzombie.com/hudson-valley-zombie-apocolypse

Please visit and "Like" Linda Zimmermann's author page at:

https://www.facebook.com/Linda-Zimmermann-116636310250/